S.O.S

Spotlight on Standards!
Interactive Science Content Reader

California
Science

GRADE 4 Table of Contents

Printed in the United States of America

ISBN-13: 978-0-15-365364-3
ISBN-10: 0-15-365364-7

12 13 14 15 0877 17 16

4500587656

Standard Set 1   Physical Science

Unit 1   Electricity and Magnetism

1 Electricity and magnetism are related effects that have many useful applications in everyday life.

Electricity and Magnetism

In this unit, you'll learn about static electricity, circuits, magnetic poles, and electromagnets. You'll also learn how to detect magnetic fields, and how electricity and electromagnets are used.

☁ Thinking Ahead

What experience have you had with static electricity?

_____

_____

What does an electric circuit look like? Draw what you think.

If you heard the word electromagnet, what would you think it was made of?

_____

Look at the electrical appliances below. Tell whether you think they make heat, light, or motion.

_____ _____ _____

Write a question you have about electricity and magnetism.

_____

_____

Recording What You Learn

◄ On this page, record what you learn as you read the unit.

Lesson 1

Look at the electrically charged particles. Draw arrows to show whether they attract or repel each other. The first one is done for you.

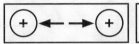 

Lesson 2

Draw a parallel circuit in the space below.

Lessons 3 and 4

How does a compass use magnetic energy to tell direction?

_____

_____

Lessons 5 and 6

Sequence the statements from 1 to 5 to tell how an electromagnet makes a doorbell work.

_____ The clapper vibrates back and forth.

_____ As the current switches direction, the electromagnet first attracts the clapper.

_____ The bell rings.

_____ When the doorbell button is pushed, current flows through the wire.

_____ Then the electromagnet repels the clapper.

Lesson 7

Name three electrical appliances in your house. One should convert electricity to heat, another to light, and the third to motion.

Light: Heat: Motion:

_____   _____   _____

1.e *Students know* electrically charged objects attract or repel each other.

Vocabulary Activity

Adjectives

When two words appear together as one term, the first word acts as an adjective. It describes the second word. Fill in the chart with your vocabulary words. An example is done for you.

Adjective	Word decribed
electric	charge

VOCABULARY

electric charge
static electricity
electric field

What Is Static Electricity?

A plus sign or a minus sign stands for an **electric charge**. Matter can have either a positive (plus sign) or a negative (minus sign) electric charge. Some matter does not have either charge.

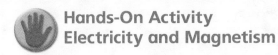
1. Demonstrate static electricity. Show what you know about positive and negative charges.

2. How did you demonstrate?

_____

_____

3. Draw a picture of what happened during your demonstration.

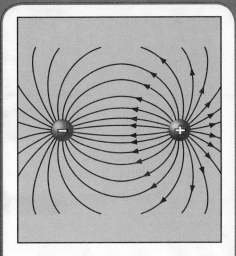

This girl has a buildup of electric charges in one place. This is why the socks stick to her sweater. Such a buildup is called **static electricity**.

The area around an electric charge is called the **electric field**. It is where electric forces act.

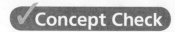

1. A **Cause** makes something happen. An **Effect** is the thing that happens. Circle one cause of charges being attracted to each other. Underline an effect of the same charges being near each other.

2. Draw boxes around two types of charges that particles in matter can have.

_____

3. Why is matter usually neutral?

_____

_____

Two Kinds of Charge

You already know the word *electricity*. Electricity is a kind of energy. This energy depends on properties of matter. Many of the tiny particles that make up matter have an **electric charge**. These charges can be positive or negative.

Positive and negative charges can cancel each other out. Matter is usually *neutral*, not positive or negative. The charges are usually in balance.

Rubbing the balloon causes a charge.

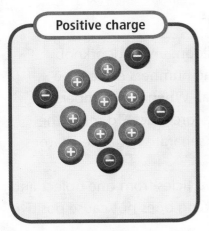

Positive charge

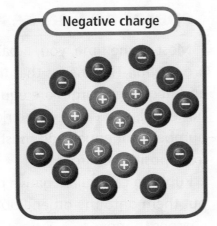

Negative charge

Positively charged objects and negatively charged objects affect each other. Opposite charges attract, or pull toward each other. Charges that are the same repel, or push away from each other.

The buildup of charges in one place is called **static electricity**. When clothes rub against each other in the dryer, they cause static electricity.

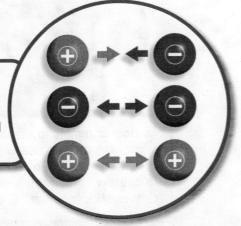

Objects that have the same charge push away from each other. Objects with different charges pull toward each other.

1. What causes static electricity?

_____

2. Look at the picture of the charges below. Circle the pair of charges that attract.

3. Use arrows to show how the charges below will move.

4. What is the effect of clothes rubbing against each other in the dryer?

_____

1. A **Cause** makes something happen. An **Effect** is the thing that happens. Circle a cause of objects being neutral. Underline an effect of unequal charges on an object.

2. When two objects are rubbed together, what kind of particle gets moved from one to the other?

_____

_____

Separating Charges

Most of the time, you, a balloon, and a doorknob are *neutral*. This means that the numbers of positive and negative charges are equal. When the numbers are not equal, you can see electric forces act. To make the numbers not equal, you must separate negative charges from positive charges.

Rubbing can pull negative particles from one object and put them onto the other. Rubbing does not cause positive charges to move.

As clothes tumble in the dryer, different fabrics rub against one another. Negative charges move from one piece of clothing to another. When this happens, the clothes stick together.

What causes a negatively charged balloon to stick to a neutral wall? This happens because there is another way to separate charges. The balloon's negative charges repel negative charges in the wall. The wall's negative charges move away a little. They are now separated from the wall's positive charges. The balloon's negative charges are then attracted to the wall's positive charges. The balloon sticks to the wall.

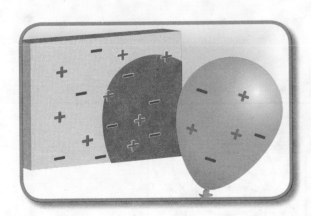

◄ The balloon is neutral. It has the same number of positive and negative charges.

The balloon is negatively charged. The negative charges on the wall are pushed away. The balloon is attracted to the wall's positive charges. It sticks to the wall. ►

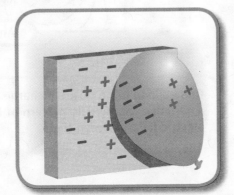

✓ Concept Check

1. What are two ways you can cause charges to separate?

_____

_____

2. Show the steps that cause a negatively charged balloon to stick to a neutral wall.

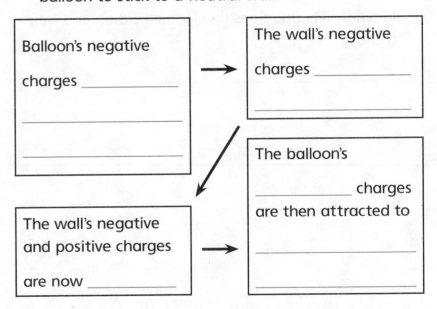

Balloon's negative charges _____

_____

→

The wall's negative charges _____

_____

The balloon's _____ charges are then attracted to _____

_____

The wall's negative and positive charges are now _____

→

3. Circle the picture that shows a balloon that is negatively charged.

1. A **Cause** makes something happen. An **Effect** is the thing that happens. Circle the picture that shows the effect of two negatively charged balloons being near each other.

2. What is an electric field?

_____

3. In what direction does an electric field extend from a charge?

_____

Electric Forces

Positive and negative electric charges have electric fields around them. An **electric field** is the space in which an electric force acts. An electric field extends in all directions from the charge. A positive charge's field attracts any nearby negative charge. It repels any nearby positive charge.

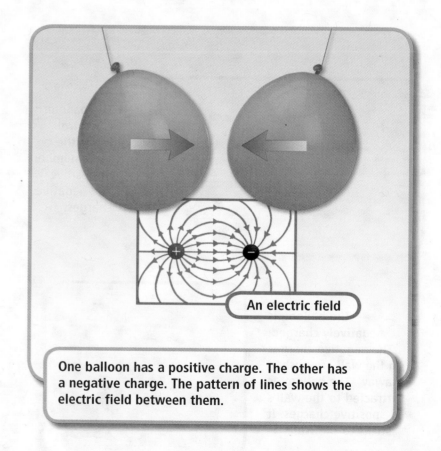

An electric field

One balloon has a positive charge. The other has a negative charge. The pattern of lines shows the electric field between them.

The diagram on this page shows what the electric fields around two negatively charged balloons look like. The lines show that the balloons repel each other.

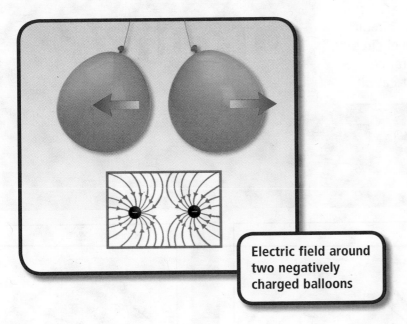

Electric field around two negatively charged balloons

Complete the following Cause and Effect statements.

1. An _____ _____ is a property of some matter.

2. Charges can be _____ or _____.

3. The buildup of charges in one place is called _____ _____.

4. An _____ _____ is the space in which an electric force acts.

1.a *Students know* how to design and build simple series and parallel circuits by using components such as wires, batteries, and bulbs.

Vocabulary Activity

It's Electric!

How does electricity flow from one place to another? You'll find out in this lesson.

1. Look at the vocabulary words. How many different kinds of circuits will you learn about in this lesson?

_____

2. Write a sentence using the term *electric current*.

_____

_____

Lesson **2**

What Makes a Circuit?

VOCABULARY

electric current
electric circuit
series circuit
parallel circuit
resistance
short circuit

An **electric current** brings electric energy to light the bulb.

The bulb lights because it has a steady flow of electric current. The continuous pathway is called an **electric circuit**.

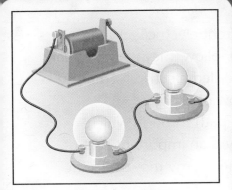

Both bulbs light because there is one path that allows current to flow. This is called a **series circuit**.

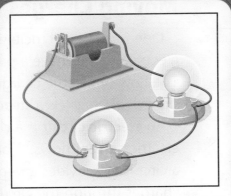

A **parallel circuit** has two or more paths where current can flow. If one bulb goes out, the others stay on.

The filament in this light bulb has a high **resistance**. This means it reduces the flow of electric current.

In this picture, electricity is flowing where it should not. That creates a **short circuit**.

Hands-On Activity
Series or Parallel Circuits?

You can find parallel and series circuits in your home.

1. Ask a parent or guardian if you have a string of holiday or patio lights in your home. Remove one light from the string and plug in the string. Does it still work?

_____

2. What kind of circuit do the lights use?

_____

3. How would the outcome have changed if the lights were the other type of circuit?

_____

_____

_____

1. A **Cause** makes something happen. An **Effect** is the thing that happens. Circle the object that causes electric charges to move through a circuit.

2. Look at the picture of the circuit on this page. Use arrows to show how the current flows.

3. How is an electric current different from an electric circuit?

_____

_____

_____

Moving Charges

One form of electricity is current electricity. When electric charges have a path to follow, they move, or *flow*. The flow of electric charges is called **electric current**. *Current electricity* is a steady flow of charges.

An **electric circuit** is a closed path through which electric current flows. A battery is an important part of a circuit. It provides energy. The energy moves electric charges through the circuit.

▲ Trace the path of the current through each part of the circuit.

Current flows through the circuit below. It flows like water through the trays of the fountain. You control a fountain by closing off a pipe. You control the path of current electricity by opening a switch. This breaks the path of the current flow.

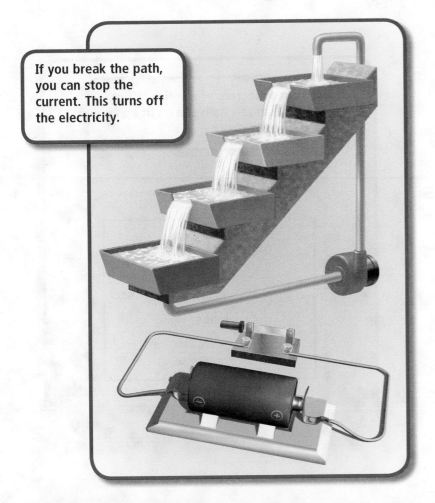

If you break the path, you can stop the current. This turns off the electricity.

✓ Concept Check

1. Underline the sentence that tells how you control the path of current electricity.

2. Look at the picture. How is the waterfall similar to an electric circuit?

_____

_____

3. Look at the picture of the circuit on this page. What could you do to break the path of current flow?

_____

_____

1. A **Cause** makes something happen. An **Effect** is the thing that happens. Circle a sentence that gives a cause of lights in a series circuit not working.

2. What is a series circuit?

_____

_____

3. Label the parts of the series circuit on page 15. Use arrows to draw the path of current flow.

4. What happens to an electric current after it passes through each bulb?

_____

Series Circuits

A **series circuit** has only one path for current to follow. It's like riding on a Ferris wheel. You have to go all the way around to get back to the start.

A series circuit can have more than one bulb. The electric current moves from the battery through the wire. It passes through each bulb. Then it returns to the battery.

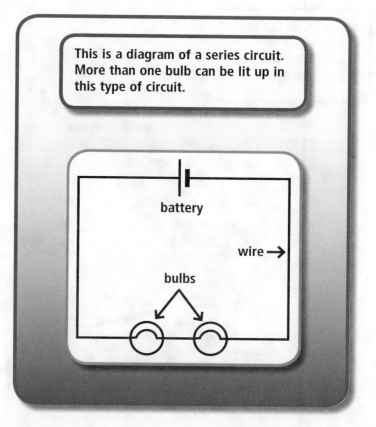

This is a diagram of a series circuit. More than one bulb can be lit up in this type of circuit.

battery

wire →

bulbs

In a series circuit, taking out any part stops the flow of electricity. The bulb will not light. Current flows only when everything is connected.

A series circuit works well in a simple device such as a flashlight. You would not use a series circuit for your whole home. To make one light work, you'd have to turn them all on!

This is a series circuit. If you took out one light bulb, all the lights would go out.

1. How does a series circuit turn off?

_____

2. Fill in the chart. Write "yes" if a series circuit is a good idea, write "no" if a series circuit is not a good idea.

Device	Good or Bad?
Flashlight	
Lights for whole home	
A string of lights	
A simple lamp with one bulb	

3. Why doesn't a series circuit work well in your whole home?

_____

_____

1. A **Cause** makes something happen. An **Effect** is the thing that happens. Circle the cause that allows people to turn devices on a parallel circuit on or off at different times.

2. You have three devices turned on along a parallel circuit. If you remove one device, what happens to the others?

   _____

3. Look at the picture of the parallel circuit. Circle the part that makes it different from a series circuit.

4. What can cause the flow of electricity to slow down?

   _____

Parallel Circuits

A better way to wire your home is to use parallel circuits. A **parallel circuit** has more than one path for the current to follow. If something blocks one path, the charges can flow along another path. At least one light stays lit.

In a parallel circuit, the current splits among different paths. People can turn devices on or off at different times. Plugging in more devices does not change how the circuit works.

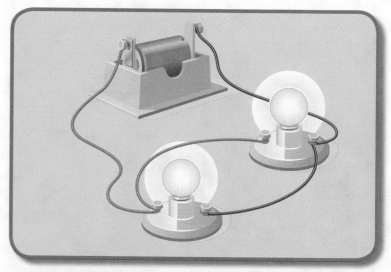

▲ This is a parallel circuit. There is more than one path for the current to flow along. You can block one path, or remove a bulb. The other bulbs will still light.

Resistance

The flow of electricity is like car traffic. If there are many lanes, cars can move easily. If cars must share one lane, traffic slows down. The amount of current that can flow through a circuit depends on resistance. **Resistance** is how much a material slows down the flow.

Sometimes a wrong connection is made. The current takes a shortcut. The shortcut is called a **short circuit**. In a short circuit, current flows where it isn't wanted. Short circuits prevent the rest of a circuit from working properly.

Lesson Review

Complete the following Cause and Effect statements.

1. A battery moves energy through an _____.

2. If one light is disconnected in a _____ circuit, they all go out.

3. A _____ circuit allows current to flow along more than one path.

4. _____ slows down the flow of current.

1.f *Students know* that magnets have two poles (north and south) and that like poles repel each other while unlike poles attract each other.

Vocabulary Activity

Magnetism

This lesson focuses on magnets, and what makes them work.

1. The word magnet comes from an old French word *magnete,* which meant stone. What do you think magnets are made of?

_____

_____

Do some research to see if you are right.

2. Look at the terms *magnetic poles* and *magnetic fields.* Just by looking at the terms, what do you think these poles and fields have in common?

_____

_____

 Lesson **3**

What Are Magnetic Poles?

VOCABULARY

magnet
magnetic poles
magnetic field

A **magnet** attracts iron and some other metals. This large magnet attracts a paper clip through three sheets of paper.

18

© Harcourt

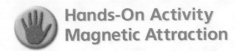
1. Find a magnet. Test things with your magnet. See how many things are attracted to it.

2. List things that are attracted to your magnet and things that are not.

Things that are attracted	Things that are NOT attracted

3. What conclusion could you draw about what a magnet attracts?

_____

_____

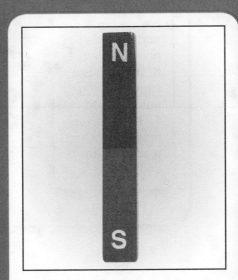

The metal filings are affected by the magnet. They show where the **magnetic field** is located.

Every magnet has two **magnetic poles**. The N and S ends of the magnet are where it can pull with the largest force.

1. The **Main Idea** of these two pages is <u>Magnets have two different poles</u>. **Details** tell more about the main idea. Underline two details about how the poles affect attraction between magnets.

2. Look at the magnet below. Circle the end that will point north if you hang it. Draw an arrow to the pole that will point south.

3. What is usually in materials that are attracted to magnets?

_____

4. What are the ends of a magnet called?

_____

Two Poles

A **magnet** is an object that attracts certain materials. These materials usually contain iron. The two ends of a magnet are called **magnetic poles**. The magnetic force is strongest near the two poles.

When you hang a bar magnet and let it turn, one end points north. This end is called the *north-seeking pole* (N). The other end is the *south-seeking pole* (S).

A magnet always has a north-seeking pole, labeled N. It also has a south-seeking pole, labeled S. If you cut a magnet, each piece still has N and S poles.

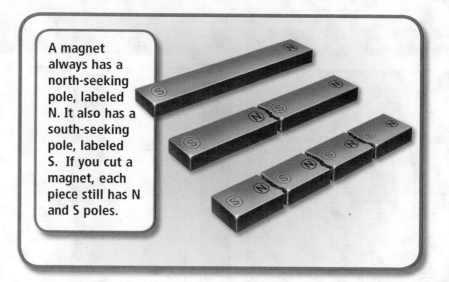

© Harcourt

Magnetic poles act like electric charges. Opposite poles attract. Same poles repel. Opposite poles placed near each other will pull toward each other. When same poles are placed near each other, they push apart.

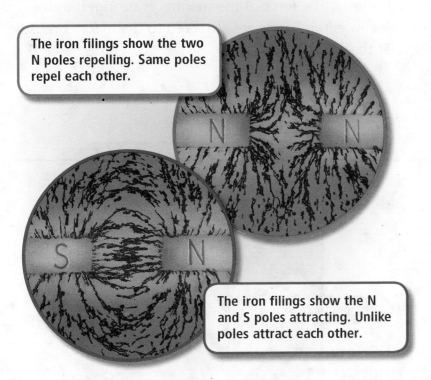

The iron filings show the two N poles repelling. Same poles repel each other.

The iron filings show the N and S poles attracting. Unlike poles attract each other.

1. Write two ways magnetic poles act like electrical charges.

   1. _____

   2. _____

2. Write two ways magnets are alike.

   1. _____

   2. _____

3. In the space below, draw two magnets that repel each other. Label the magnetic poles.

4. Fill in the chart. Tell if iron filings will be attracted and connect or repelled and move away.

Magnetic poles	What happnes to iron filings between them?
S – S	
N – S	
S – N	
N – N	

1. The **Main Idea** of these two pages is <u>Magnets have different shapes and magnetic fields</u>. **Details** tell more about the main idea. Underline one detail about magnetic fields, and one about different magnet shapes.

2. On the pictures below, circle the places where the force is strongest.

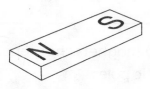 

3. Why do magnets have different shapes?

_____

4. What do the iron filings in the picture show?

_____

_____

Magnetic Forces

A **magnetic field** is the area in which the magnetic force of a magnet acts. In the picture, a bar magnet moves iron filings into a shape. The shape shows the magnet's magnetic field. Lines form between the N and S poles of the magnet. These lines are called magnetic field lines. They show lines of magnetic force.

Magnetic force gets stronger as the magnetic object gets closer. The force of the magnet is strongest at the poles. The iron filings are attracted to the magnet mostly near the poles.

magnetic field

Magnet Shapes

Magnets come in many shapes and sizes. They are made for different uses. Some are shaped like horseshoes. If you straightened the horseshoe out, the poles would be at the ends. You might have a flat rubber magnet at home. These magnets are made up of stripes of magnetic material. The material bends.

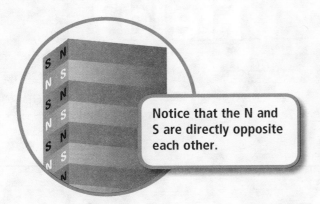

Notice that the N and S are directly opposite each other.

Complete this Main Idea statement.

1. A _____ is the place on a magnet where the force is strongest.

Complete these Detail statements about magnets.

2. A _____ is an object that attracts iron and some other metals.

3. The space in which the magnetic force acts around a magnet is called the _____.

4. Even if a magnet has different shapes, it will always have a _____ and a _____ pole.

How Can You Detect a Magnetic Field?

California Standards in This Lesson

 I.b *Students know* how to build a simple compass and use it to detect magnetic effects, including Earth's magnetic field.

Vocabulary Activity

Compass

How can you find magnetic fields? You can use a compass.

1. The word *compass* comes from the old French word *compasser*, meaning "to measure." What do you think the word *compass* means?

_____

_____

2. Which device converts electrical energy to kinetic energy?

stove　　　**lightbulb**　　　**insulator**　　　**electric motor**

A **compass** helps you find directions. It tells you which way is north.

Hands-On Activity
Using a Compass

You can use a compass to find direction.

1. Take a compass outside of your house, or your school. Find where north, south, east, and west are.

2. Make a map in the space below. Show either your home or school, and a legend pointing the directions north, south, east, and west.

3. Return to the same spot at sundown. The sun will set in the west. Check your map against the sunset. Were your directions correct?

1. A **Cause** makes something happen. An **Effect** is the thing that happens. Circle the cause of Earth's magnetic poles. Underline an effect that Earth's magnetic field could have on a magnet.

2. In the box below, Earth is shown as if it is cut in half. Label Earth's giant magnet and its magnetic north pole and magnetic south pole. Draw arrows from the labels to the things they tell about.

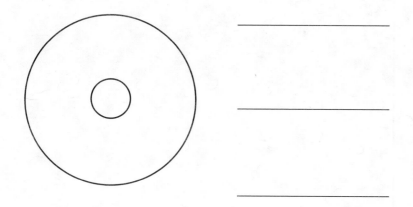

Finding the North Pole

Earth has a North pole and a South pole. You might think of them as the "top" and "bottom" points of Earth. They are the imaginary points that do not move as Earth rotates. Earth's core is a huge magnet. Because of this, Earth also has magnetic poles. It has a giant magnetic field.

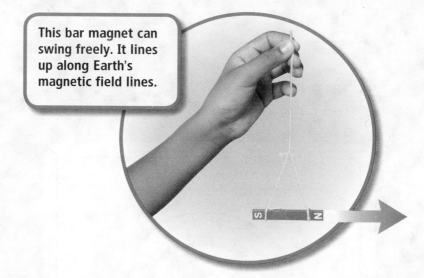

This bar magnet can swing freely. It lines up along Earth's magnetic field lines.

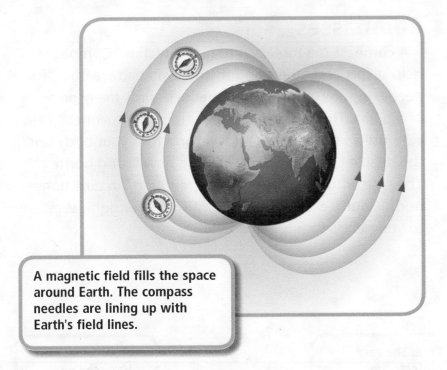

A magnetic field fills the space around Earth. The compass needles are lining up with Earth's field lines.

A magnetic field fills the space around Earth. You saw the way iron filings lined up around a magnet. They showed that the magnetic field was strongest at the magnet's poles. This is also true of Earth's poles. A magnet hanging near one of Earth's poles would line up with the field. It would point into the ground.

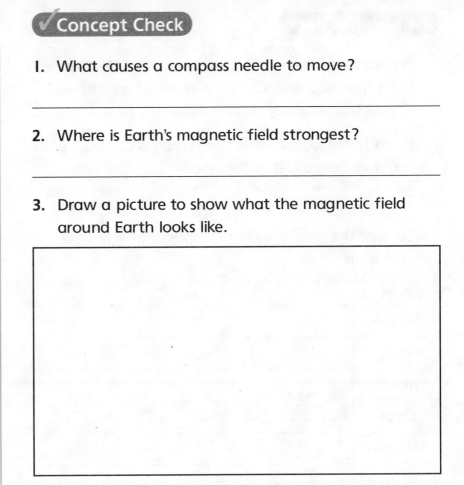

✓ Concept Check

1. What causes a compass needle to move?

_____

2. Where is Earth's magnetic field strongest?

_____

3. Draw a picture to show what the magnetic field around Earth looks like.

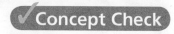
1. A **Cause** makes something happen. An **Effect** is the thing that happens. Circle the cause of a compass needle lining up with Earth's magnetic field.

2. What might be the effect of having a compass with you if you were lost in the woods?

_____

3. Look at the picture of the compass. Tell what each part does.

Part	Job
Case	
Pivot	
Needle	
Liquid	
Markings	

4. How can magnets cause problems with the way a compass works?

_____

_____

Compasses

A **compass** is a tool used to find direction. Compasses help sailors and others find their way in bad weather. The needle in the compass is magnetic. It turns freely on top of a point. The needle lines up with Earth's magnetic field.

To use a compass, hold it level and turn your body until the needle points at the N. You are now facing north. The face of the compass shows the four main directions—north, south, east, and west. East is to your right. West is to your left. South is behind you.

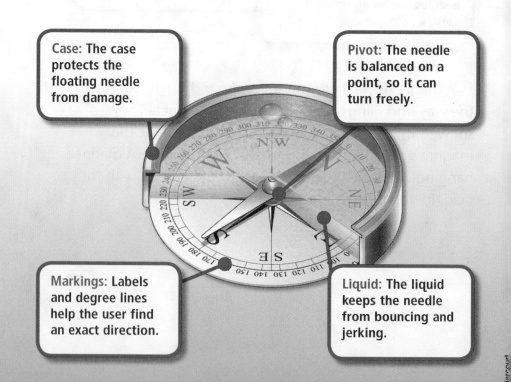

Case: The case protects the floating needle from damage.

Pivot: The needle is balanced on a point, so it can turn freely.

Markings: Labels and degree lines help the user find an exact direction.

Liquid: The liquid keeps the needle from bouncing and jerking.

Magnetic Interference

Magnets or large metal objects interfere with a compass. If they are nearby, the compass may not work correctly. The best place to use a compass is outdoors. Stay away from other magnets, buildings, power lines, and cars, and your compass will work correctly.

The compass is not pointing to Earth's magnetic north. It is pointing to the magnet instead. ▶

Complete the following Cause and Effect statements.

1. Earth's core acts like a giant _____.

2. A compass needle turns to line up along _____ magnetic field lines.

3. If you are lost, a _____ is a tool that can help you find your way.

4. _____ or _____ can interfere with the way a compass works.

I.c *Students know* electric currents produce magnetic fields and know how to build a simple electromagnet.

Vocabulary Activity

Electromagnet

What happens when you combine the words *electricity* and *magnetism*? You get the word *electromagnet*.

1. The chart shows the two words that are the base words for electromagnet. Then think of two other words that, combined, make new words. Add them to the chart.

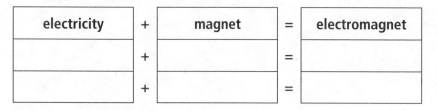

electricity	+	magnet	=	electromagnet
	+		=	
	+		=	

VOCABULARY
electromagnet

What Makes an Electromagnet?

1. Make your own magnet. Rub a paper clip with a magnet 25 times in the same direction. Put a piece of foam in a bowl of water. Put the paper clip on top of the foam. Watch to see what the paper clip does. Move the bowl. What happens to the paper clip?

_____

_____

2. Make your own electromagnet with household wires. Look at the caption on the photo for clues.

3. Write the steps you will follow.

   1. _____

   2. _____

You can make an **electromagnet** with a nail, some covered wire, and a battery. The wire will carry current. The nail will become a magnet.

1. The **Main Idea** on these two pages is <u>An electromagnet combines electricity and magnetism.</u> **Details** tell more about the main idea. Underline two details about how an electromagnet is made.

2. What do electric charges and magnetic forces have in common?

   _____

3. Look at the iron fillings in the picture of the coil. What do they show?

   _____

4. If you put iron filings near a wire, nothing happens. What must you do to make something happen?

   _____

Making a Magnetic Field

You know that electric charges can push or pull. Magnets also have a force that can push or pull. Are magnetism and electricity related?

Nothing happens when you put iron filings near a copper wire. Now run a current through the wire. A weak magnetic field forms. The picture shows a wire coil that carries a current. Notice what the iron fillings show. It is the shape of the magnetic field inside the coil.

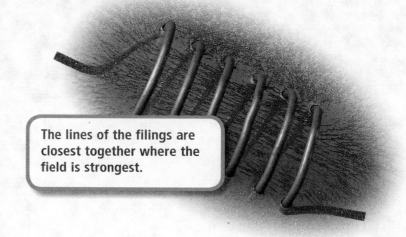

The lines of the filings are closest together where the field is strongest.

Electric current from the battery runs through the wire around the iron nail. The current makes the nail magnetic. Taking out the battery stops the current. The iron filings would no longer stick to the nail.

The magnetic field around a current-carrying wire can move a compass needle. You can make the field stronger. You can wrap the wire around a core, such as a nail.

You can make an **electromagnet**. Wrap a coil of wire around an iron nail. Attach a battery to the wire. The nail becomes a magnet when electric current flows in the wire. The nail is a magnet only when current is flowing.

✓ Concept Check

1. Cross out the object that is NOT used to make an electromagnet.

2. Fill in the numbered steps. Show how to make an electromagnet.

   1. _____

   2. _____

   3. _____

   _____

3. What turns the iron nail into a magnet?

   _____

1. The **Main Idea** on these two pages is
   <u>Electromagnets can be controlled</u>. **Details** tell about
   the main idea. Underline two details that tell how
   electromagnets can be controlled.

2. Look at the picture of the two electromagnets.
   Circle the stronger one. Then tell what makes
   it stronger.

   _____

3. Write two ways to make an electromagnet stronger.

   1. _____

   2. _____

4. An electromagnet has one battery. Another
   electromagnet has two batteries. Which
   electromagnet is stronger?

   _____

Controlling Electromagnets

An electromagnet is a *temporary* magnet. You can turn
it on and off. How could a magnet like this be useful? A
powerful electromagnet can pick up tons of iron scrap.
A worker could turn on the electromagnet to pick up the
iron. The worker simply turns off the electromagnet to
drop the iron.

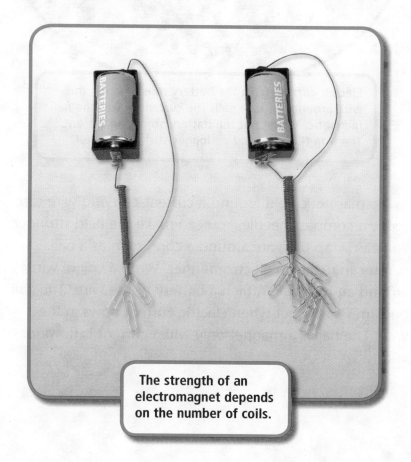

The strength of an
electromagnet depends
on the number of coils.

© Harcourt

There are two ways to make an electromagnet stronger. One is by adding more coils. The other is increasing the electric current. For example, you could add more batteries.

We use electromagnets in many ways. They are found everywhere. Some are inside your telephone. Some are outside at the automobile junkyard!

This electromagnet is stronger because it uses two batteries.

Complete this Main Idea statement.

1. An _____ is a magnet that has coils of current-carrying wire around an iron core.

Complete these Detail statements.

2. An electromagnet is a _____ magnet. It can be turned on and off.

3. Magnets produce a force that can push or _____, just as electric charges can.

4. The strength of an electromagnet depends on the number of its _____.

I.d *Students know* the role of electromagnets in the construction of electric motors, electric generators, and simple devices such as doorbells and earphones.

Vocabulary Activity

Using Electromagnets

In this lesson, you'll read about how electromagnets are used. Knowing these vocabulary words will make the lesson easier to understand.

1. *Kinetic energy* and *electric motor* are terms whose first word describes the second. Fill in the blanks.

Kinetic energy is a type of _____.

An electric motor is a type of _____.

2. The word *generator* comes from the verb *generate*, which means "to produce or bring into being." Tell what you think a generator is.

_____

_____

Lesson **6**

How Are Electromagnets Used?

This wind farm is changing **kinetic energy**, or energy of motion, to electricity.

© Harcourt

A small toy car has a small **electric motor**. The motor makes it move.

People use portable **generators** when their power goes out.

1. Look through the lesson and find one way electromagnets are used. Draw it here.

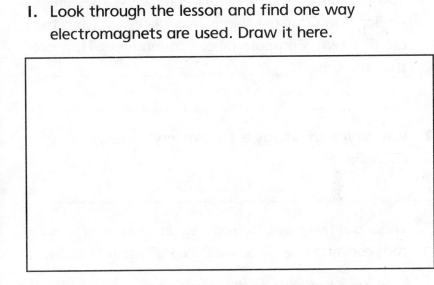

2. Label each part of the electromagnet in your picture.

1. You **Compare** things by looking for ways they are similar. You **Contrast** things by looking for ways they are different. Compare all electromagnets. How are they the same? _____

   _____

2. What type of energy is the battery's energy changed to?

   _____

3. There are five steps for making an electromagnet that converts energy to motion. Put them in order.

   _____ Leave the ends of the wire free.

   _____ Now attach the ends of the wire to a battery.

   _____ The nail will move!

   _____ Take a plastic drinking straw and wrap many coils of wire around it.

   _____ Lay the straw on the table, and slide an iron nail partway inside.

Electromagnetism and Motion

You can create a device that changes battery electricity into motion. Take a plastic drinking straw and wrap many coils of wire around it. Leave the ends of the wire free. Lay the straw on the table, and slide an iron nail partway inside. Now attach the ends of the wire to a battery. The nail will move! The magnetic field inside the coil produces a force. The force moves the nail.

This device changes energy from the battery to motion. Energy of motion is called **kinetic energy**.

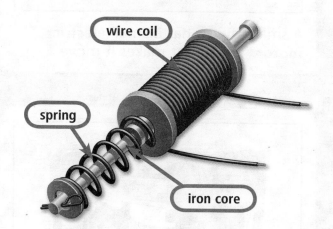

wire coil

spring

iron core

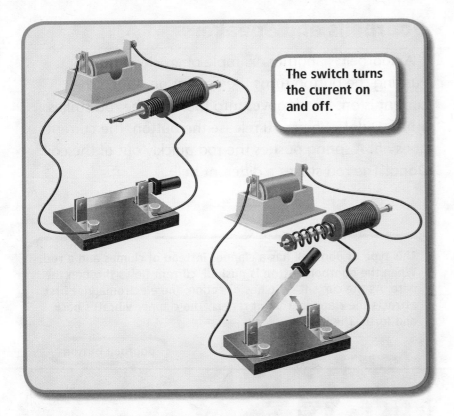

The switch turns the current on and off.

The device in the picture works the same way the nail in the straw did. Turning the current on and off produces motion, or kinetic energy.

Changing electricity to kinetic energy is useful. One way is in starting a car. The driver turns the key. This closes a switch. A tiny current travels through a relay. The relay closes a switch in a different circuit. The relay moves a rod to touch another piece of metal. Now electricity can flow and start the car.

1. What is kinetic energy?

_____

2. How is kinetic energy from an electromagnet useful?

_____

3. Fill in the blanks in the sequence boxes. Tell how an electromagnet can start a car.

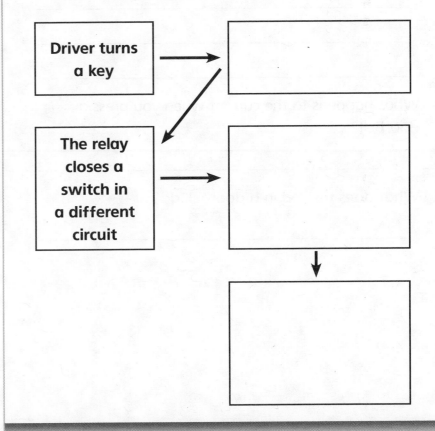

1. You **Compare** things by looking for ways they are similar. You **Contrast** things by looking for ways they are different. Compare and contrast doorbells and headphones.

_____

_____

_____

_____

2. What happens to the current when you press a doorbell?

_____

3. What does the rod in a doorbell do?

_____

Doorbells and Speakers

A doorbell is another example of an electromagnet. Pushing the button turns the current on. When the current is on, a rod moves into the coil. The rod strikes a bell. Ding! When you release the button, the current goes off. A spring pushes the rod quickly out of the coil. Dong! The rod strikes a different bell.

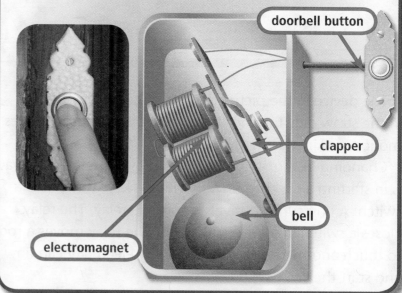

This type of doorbell has a clapper instead of chimes and a rod. When the doorbell button is pushed, current flows through the wire. As the current switches direction, the electromagnet first attracts the clapper. Then it repels. The clapper vibrates back and forth. The bell rings.

doorbell button

clapper

bell

electromagnet

Speakers and headphones also use electromagnets. Microphones change sounds into electrical signals. When the signals reach a speaker, they are turned back into sounds.

Every speaker has a flexible diaphragm. The diaphragm is attached to a magnet. A wire coil wraps around the magnet. Electrical signals pass through the coil. This causes the coil to push and pull on the magnet. The diaphragm vibrates, causing sound waves. You hear the music!

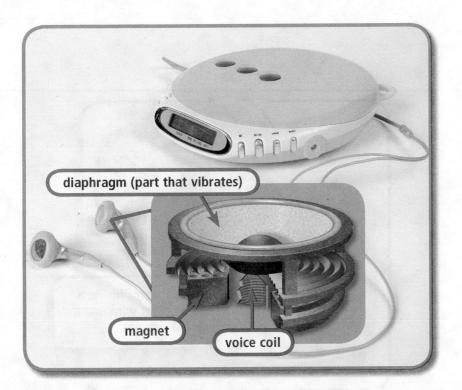

diaphragm (part that vibrates)

magnet

voice coil

1. Explain how sound moves from a microphone into speakers.

_____

_____

2. What happens when electric signals pass through the coil in a speaker?

_____

3. Fill in the blanks in the sequence boxes. Tell how an electromagnet is used by speakers.

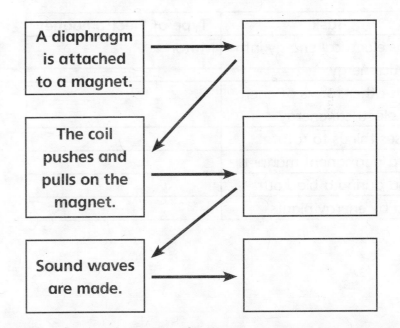

A diaphragm is attached to a magnet.	→	
The coil pushes and pulls on the magnet.	→	
Sound waves are made.	→	

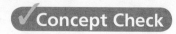

1. You **Compare** things by looking for ways they are similar. You **Contrast** things by looking for ways they are different.

   Compare and contrast electric motors and generators.

   _____

   _____

   _____

2. Fill in the chart. Tell what type of electromagnet does each job. The first one is done for you.

Task	Type of Electromagnet
Turns electrical energy into kinetic energy	Motor
Turns other forms of energy into electrical energy	
Causes things to rotate	
Has a permanent magnet	
Good during a blackout	
Used by energy plants	

Electric Motors

Have you ever cooled off with an electric fan? A fan contains a small motor. An **electric motor** changes electrical energy into kinetic energy. Motors usually cause things to rotate, or spin.

A simple motor has a wire coil and a permanent magnet. Current flows through the wire. The magnet pulls on the coil. The coil turns halfway. The current changes direction. Now the magnet pushes on the coil. The coil turns halfway again. This pattern repeats again and again. The motor spins.

The electric motor inside a fan has a coil of wire and a permanent magnet.

Generators

A **generator** converts other forms of energy into electrical energy. In an emergency, electricity can go out. People can get electricity by running a generator with gasoline. It can provide electricity for lights. It can provide electricity for keeping food cold.

Energy plants have huge generators that contain electromagnets. The energy plants burn fuel. The fuel heats water to change it to steam. The steam pushes against fan blades, which turn a shaft. The shaft turns electromagnets inside heavy coils of copper wire. The spinning magnets cause current in the wire.

Lesson Review

Complete the following Compare and Contrast statements.

1. Energy of motion is called_____.

2. Electrical energy can be changed into kinetic energy with an _____.

3. A _____ is a machine that converts other forms of energy into electrical energy.

4. Speakers, headphones, and doorbells use _____.

I.g *Students know* electrical energy can be converted to heat, light, and motion.

Vocabulary Activity

Insulate

You may be able to think of a few ways electrical energy is used. In this lesson, you'll see how electricity changes into light and heat, and how it makes things move.

I. There are many suffixes you can add to the word insulate. Write some of them.

_____

_____

_____

_____

VOCABULARY
insulate

How Is Electrical Energy Used?

Hands-On Activity
Insulators

1. Look around your house for objects that use electricity.

2. Make a list of the objects. Tell how each is insulated.

Object	How is it insulated?

3. Do you see any electrical objects without insulators? List them here.

_____

_____

_____

A wire is **insulated** to protect you from electric current.

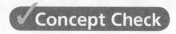
1. The **Main Idea** of these two pages is <u>Electricity is</u> <u>converted to different forms so we can use it.</u> **Details** tell more about the main idea. Circle two details about the forms into which electricity is converted.

2. What are three ways we use electricity?

_____

_____

_____

3. What do a stove burner and a lightbulb have in common?

_____

_____

Converting to Heat and Light

Can you picture a world without electricity? We use electricity every day in many ways. Today, we don't think about electricity until the power goes out. Then we realize how much we use electricity. We use it to cook, make light, and keep food cool.

Many uses of electricity make both light and heat. A stove burner produces both heat and light. The filament in a light bulb also produces light and heat.

Bumper cars use electricity to make them move.

Converting to Motion

Many devices use electricity to produce motion. For example, a hair dryer uses electricity to move air. An elevator uses electricity to move up and down. Some cars run on electricity from batteries.

Factories build cars, computers, and appliances on an assembly line. The assembly line uses electricity. So do the tools the workers use.

✓ **Concept Check**

1. In a factory, how is electricity used?

_____

2. Draw an electrical object you used today. Tell whether you used it for light, heat, or motion.

1. The **Main Idea** on these two pages is <u>Electricity can be dangerous.</u> **Details** tell more about the main idea. Circle two details about how electricity can be made safer.

2. Why does insulation protect you from electricity?

_____

3. What is an insulator?

_____

4. Why are most cords covered with plastic?

_____

Electrical Safety

Electricity can be very dangerous. Touching wires that carry electric current can cause serious injury. This is why electrical devices must be insulated. To **insulate** means to protect from electricity. Insulation is a material that does not carry current.

Plastic is a good insulator. Outlet covers, cords and plugs are covered with plastic. This protects people from the electric current. When you plug in something, hold only the insulated plug. Never pull on the cord to unplug the device.

◄ Remove a cord by holding onto the plug.

◄ Do not pull on a cord. This could break the insulation. The electricity could shock you.

A microwave oven uses a lot of current. So does a space heater. When a lot of current flows through wires, they become very hot. These devices have thicker wires with thicker insulation. These wires stay cooler.

Home wires can carry only a certain amount of current. Plugging more than three devices into one socket is dangerous. Too much current may flow. The wires could overheat and cause a fire. Use a power strip instead.

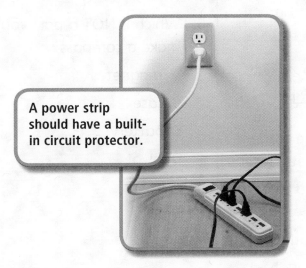

A power strip should have a built-in circuit protector.

Complete the following Main Idea statement.

1. We use _____ in many ways every day.

Complete the following detail statements.

2. Light bulbs change electricity to _____ and _____.

3. Electric motors can produce _____ in devices such as a car or a ceiling fan.

4. Electric wires are _____, or covered, to protect people from dangerous electricity.

Circle the letter in front of the best choice.

1. Which is an example of static electricity?

   A clothes sticking to each other

   B charges pushing each other away

   C clothes repelling each other

   D charges repelling each other

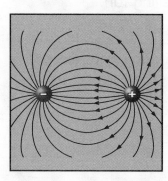

2. What does this diagram show?

   A two charges repelling

   B an electric force

   C an electric field

   D a force field

3. Which is TRUE of a parallel circuit?

   A It is powered by magnetism.

   B It has high resistance.

   C If one bulb goes out, they all do.

   D If one bulb goes out, the others stay on.

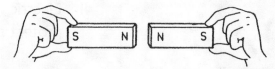

4. What will happen as the student moves these two magnets closer?

   A They will be attracted to each other.

   B They will repel each other.

   C A current will run through them.

   D They will become magnetically neutral.

5. What tool helps you detect Earth's magnetic field?

   A magnetic shield

   B compass

   C electromagnet

   D series circuit

6. Which is NOT a part you need to make a compass?

   A magnet

   B case

   C battery

   D pivot

7. Which is TRUE of electromagnets?

   A They are not real magnets.

   B You do not need a current to make them.

   C A magnet is used to make an electric field.

   D A current is used to make a magnetic field.

8. All of these parts are needed to make an electromagnet EXCEPT

   A a magnet.

   B an iron nail.

   C a coil.

   D a battery.

9. Which machine uses an electromagnet to make electricity?

   A motor

   B kinetic device

   C headphones

   D generator

10. Some electric devices convert electricity to

    A water.

    B air.

    C heat.

    D darkness.

11. Which device converts electrical energy to kinetic energy?

    A stove

    B light bulb

    C insulator

    D electric motor

12. What is a good insulator?

    A water

    B sugar

    C corn meal

    D plastic

13. What does a motor do?

    _____

    _____

14. Look back to the question you wrote in your Study Journal. Do you have an answer for your question? Tell what you learned that helps you understand electricity and magnetism.

    _____

    _____

    _____

    _____

Electricity and Magnetism

In this unit you will learn about food chains and food webs, and how living things compete for resources. What do you know about these topics? What questions do you have?

☁ Thinking Ahead

What do wild animals eat? Draw some food sources here, and show the animals that eat them.

What might happen if too many animals moved into an area?

_____

Write a question you have about how living things get energy to survive and grow.

_____

_____

_____

Finish the food chain below by drawing what squirrels eat.

Recording What You Learn

◀ On this page, record what you learn as you read the unit.

Lesson 1

Label the carnivore, the herbivore, and the producer.

_____   _____   _____

Lesson 2

Explain what happens to a wild animal's body after the animal dies.

_____

_____

Lesson 3

Number the living things below, starting with 1, to put the food chain in order. Remember, every food chain starts with producers.

_____   _____   _____

Lesson 4

What happens when too many living things live in the same habitat? How do they get the resources they need?

_____

_____

2.a *Students know* plants are the primary source of matter and energy entering most food chains.

 2.b *Students know* producers and consumers (herbivores, carnivores, omnivores, and decomposers) are related in food chains and food webs and may compete with each other for resources in an ecosystem.

Vocabulary Activity

Suffix *-er* and Prefixes

1. The suffix *–er* means "one who does an action." What does a producer do? What does a consumer do?

_____

2. Look and the prefixes and their meanings. Fill in the chart.

Prefix	Meaning	What do they eat?
Herbi-	Vegetation	Herbivore:
Carni-	Meat	Carnivore:
Omni-	All	Omnivore:

Lesson **1**

VOCABULARY

producer
consumer
herbivore
carnivore
omnivore

What Are Producers and Consumers?

This grass is a **producer**. It can make its own food.

This **consumer** eats other living things.

This **herbivore** eats only plants.

This **carnivore** eats only other animals.

This **omnivore** eats both plants and other animals.

1. Make 10 flashcards with different animals on them. You can draw the animals, or cut them from magazines.

2. On the back of each card, write whether the animal is a herbivore, an omnivore, or a carnivore.

3. Play with a partner. Show each other your cards, and have each other guess if the animal is a herbivore, an omnivore, or a carnivore. The partner who gets the most right wins.

4. Write about one of the animals on your cards. Tell how the animal gets the energy it needs for growth.

_____

_____

_____

1. The **Main Idea** of these two pages is <u>Most living things get energy from sunlight.</u> **Details** tell more about the main idea. Circle two details that show how living things get energy from sunlight.

2. Fill in the chart about photosynthesis.

Plants Use	Plants Make
Water	
Carbon dioxide	
Sunlight	

3. Fill in the space.

   Green plants change the sun's energy to _____ _____.

Food From the Sun

Most living things get energy from sunlight. Plants make their own food. Green plants take in water and carbon dioxide. Then, using sunlight as energy, they change these to food.

Plants change the sun's energy to chemical energy. The water and carbon dioxide combine. Sugars and oxygen are made. This process of change is called *photosynthesis* (foh•toh•SIN•thuh•sis).

Green plant parts can use energy from the sun to make food.

Animals get food energy when they eat plants.

Plant roots take in water to help make food.

Plants use some of the sugars they make through photosynthesis. Sugars are food for them. They store the rest for later. Or, animals may eat the plants. Then the animals get the stored energy.

Some plant parts, like berries, do not make energy. However, they are still food for animals.

✓ Concept Check

1. What do plants use as energy in photosynthesis?

_____

2. What happens to the sugars that plants make during photosynthesis?

_____

_____

3. Fill in the blanks to show how energy is passed on.

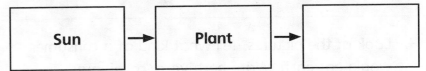

| Sun | → | Plant | → | |

4. Look at the picture of the tree. How do green plants get the water they need for photosynthesis?

_____

1. The **Main Idea** of these two pages is <u>There are producers and consumers</u>. **Details** tell more about the main idea. Circle one detail about producers and one about consumers.

2. Why are animals called consumers?

_____

3. Why are bears called omnivores?

_____

4. Look at the pictures. Tell what kind of a consumer would eat each. Write **herbivore**, **carnivore**, or **omnivore**.

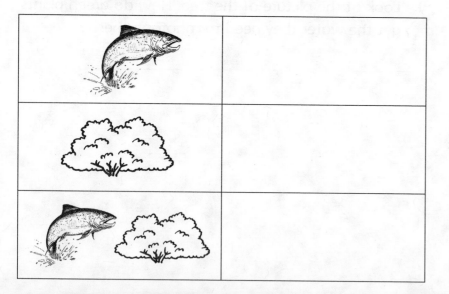

Producers and Consumers

Plants are **producers**. They make (produce) their own food. Animals are **consumers**. Consumers cannot make their own food. They must eat other living things. Deer and cattle are consumers. They eat (consume) plants. They get the energy stored in plants.

Some animals, like lions and hawks, eat other animals. Some, like horses, eat only plants. Others, like bears, eat plants and animals.

Horses eat different kinds of grasses.

Kinds of Consumers

There are three kinds of consumers. **Herbivores** eat only plants. Rabbits are herbivores. **Carnivores** eat only other animals. Lions are carnivores. **Omnivores** eat both plants and animals. Bears are omnivores.

Some producers and consumers live in water. Small herbivores, like small fish, eat algae. Omnivores, like some sea turtles, eat the small fish and larger plants. Carnivores, like larger fish, eat the smaller fish.

A sea otter is a carnivore.

Complete this Main Idea statement.

1. Plants make their own food through a process called _____.

Complete these Detail statements.

2. Plants take in carbon dioxide and _____.

3. Plants make and store _____ to use for food.

4. _____ eat plants and get food energy from them.

California Standards in This Lesson

 2.c *Students know* decomposers, including many fungi, insects, and microorganisms, recycle matter from dead plants and animals.

Vocabulary Activity

Decomposers

In this lesson, you'll learn about the organisms that help keep Earth clean.

1. The suffix *–er* means "one who does an action." What does a *scavenger* do? What does a *decomposer* do?

_____

2. The prefix *micro-* refers to things that are so small you can't see them without a microscope. Use this information to describe what microorganisms look like.

_____

_____

Lesson **2**

What Are Decomposers?

These mushrooms are **decomposers**. They are feeding off dead matter.

This **scavenger** eats other animals that have died.

60

© Harcourt

A mushroom is also a **fungus**.

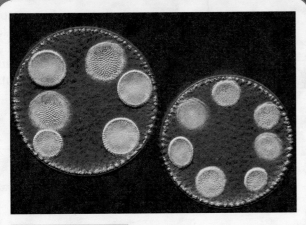

Microorganisms can only be seen under a microscope.

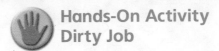

You read about how scavengers and decomposers work together to keep the balance of nature.

1. Look in a newspaper or magazine for a picture of a scavenger. Cut it out and glue or tape it in the box.

2. Write three things this scavenger eats.

    1. _____

    2. _____

    3. _____

3. How does this scavenger help nature?

    _____

    _____

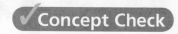

You **Compare** when you look at how things are alike. You **Contrast** when you look at how things are different.

1. Compare crows and mushrooms.

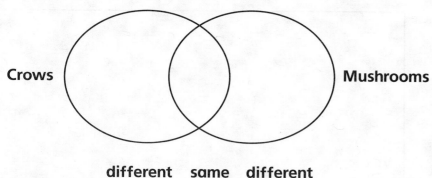

Crows   **Mushrooms**

different   same   different

2. Compare bacteria and mushroom decomposers.

_____

_____

3. What are nutrients?

_____

Decomposers

Decomposers are living things. They feed on matter from dead plants and animals. They break down wastes and remains. They turn these into *nutrients*. Nutrients are substances that living things need to grow. Decomposers return nutrients to the soil. Then they can be used again.

Bacteria are very tiny **decomposers**. Mushrooms are larger decomposers. Without decomposers, Earth would be filled with dead plants and animals.

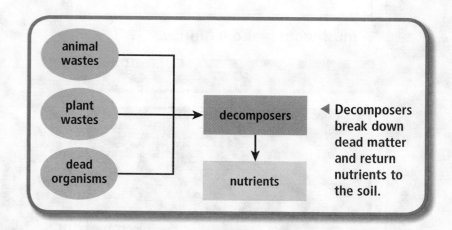

Decomposers break down dead matter and return nutrients to the soil.

A millipede eats a dead leaf.

Scavengers

Scavengers eat large pieces of plant or animal remains. These animals break the large pieces down into smaller pieces. Scavengers eat most of the dead plant or animal parts. What is left behind becomes food for decomposers.

Some birds, like crows, are scavengers. So are smaller living things like millipedes. Scavengers and decomposers work together. Both return nutrients to the soil.

This California condor is a scavenger.

✓ **Concept Check**

1. Name a scavenger.

_____

2. How do decomposers and scavengers work together?

_____

_____

_____

3. Compare and contrast scavengers and decomposers.

	Same	Different
Scavenger		
Decomposer		

You **Compare** when you look at how things are alike. You **Contrast** when you look at how things are different.

1. Compare fungi and decomposers.

_____

_____

Contrast fungi and decomposers.

_____

_____

2. What do bracket fungi feed on?

_____

3. Circle the sentence that tells how bracket fungi are helpful.

_____

Fungi

A **fungus** is a living thing that takes in nutrients. It takes nutrients from both living and dead plant matter. _Fungi_ [FUN•jy] is the plural of _fungus._

Fungi cannot make their own food. Some fungi feed on dead matter. They are decomposers. They use some of the nutrients they take in. It is their food. They return the rest to the soil.

Bracket fungi grow on dead trees. They help dead trees return nutrients to the soil.

Bracket fungi grow on dead trees. They help dead trees decay.

There are many kinds of fungi. Slime mold is a fungus. It is wet and sticky. Some mushrooms, like toadstools, are fungi. Other kinds of fungi live in fresh or salt water. Fungi are important decomposers.

Fungi are also food for other living things. Some beetles and ants eat fungi. Some people eat mushrooms. Not all mushrooms are safe to eat, though.

Puffball fungi are found on decaying wood.

Some people like morel mushrooms. They are safe to eat.

1. Fill in the chart to compare and contrast slime mold and mushroom fungi.

	Same	**Different**
Slime mold		
Mushroom fungi		

2. Where are fungi found?

_____

3. Name two uses for fungi.

   1. _____

   2. _____

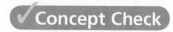

1. You **Compare** when you look at how things are alike. You **Contrast** when you look at how things are different. Fill in the chart. Check the right column to show whether each description refers to bacteria, molds, or both.

	Bacteria	Molds
Is a microorganism		
Can be a decomposer		
Are a kind of fungus		
Are foods for other living things		
Are the most common kind of microorganism		

2. Compare microorganisms to other decomposers.

_____

3. What everyday products come from mold?

_____

_____

Microorganisms

Microorganisms are among the smallest of all living things. They can be seen only under a *microscope*. Scientists use microscopes to make things look larger.

Bacteria are the most common kind of microorganism. Decomposer bacteria are found in soil and water. They break down plant and animal matter. They return nutrients to the soil or water. Other microorganisms use these nutrients for food. Then they, too, become food for other living things.

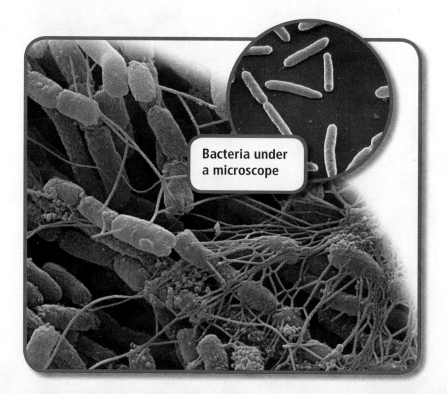

Bacteria under a microscope

Molds can also be microorganisms. They are a kind of fungus. Some are so small that you cannot see just one of them. Mold on bread is many microorganisms. Like bacteria, molds are food for other living things. Some molds help make cheese. Some molds even help make medicine.

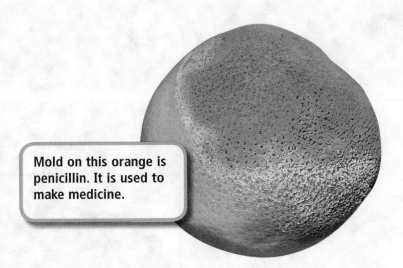

Mold on this orange is penicillin. It is used to make medicine.

Complete these Compare and Contrast statements.

1. _____ eat other animals that have died.

2. _____ like scavengers, eat dead things. But they also recycle nutrients.

3. Some _____ are used in medicine. But none can be seen without a microscope.

4. _____ are a kind of fungi that some people eat. But some kinds are not safe to eat.

2.b *Students know* producers and consumers (herbivores, carnivores, omnivores, and decomposers) are related in food chains and food webs and may compete with each other for resources in an ecosystem.

Vocabulary Activity

Food Relationships

In an ecosystem, energy moves from one living thing to another through food. You can follow the path of energy in this lesson.

I. The vocabulary terms in this lesson can be paired up. Match the terms that you think are pairs. Look for word similarities for clues.

food chain   predator

prey   food web

Lesson 3

What Are Food Chains and Food Webs?

VOCABULARY

food chain
prey
predator
food web

Energy moves from one living thing to another through food. The energy follows a **food chain**.

Some animals are hunted and eaten as **prey**.

© Harcourt

This **predator** hunts and eats other animals for food.

Some animals are part of more than one food chain. They are part of a **food web**.

Hands-On Activity
Predator and Prey

Think of five different predator-prey relationships.

1. On separate cards, draw the predator and the prey. You should make 10 cards.

2. Flip the cards over so that they are facedown.

3. Challenge a classmate to match up the pairs. He or she can turn over only one card at a time.

4. Have your classmate choose one of the pairs. Write the names of the predator and the prey.

   _____   _____

5. Write three sentences about the animals your classmate chose.

   _____

   _____

   _____

   _____

   _____

1. When you **Sequence** things, you put them in order. In the boxes below, draw the living things in a food chain. Label the consumers as **prey** and **predator** in the correct sequence.

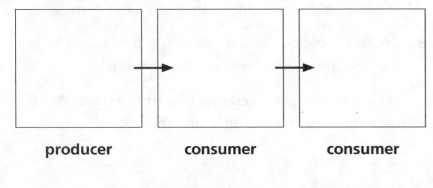

| producer | consumer | consumer |

_____ _____

2. What starts all food chains?

_____

3. What can happen after the smallest fish eat producers?

_____

4. Look at the pictures of the hawk, chipmunk, and acorn. Circle the predator. Put a box around the prey.

Food Chains

Living things need food energy to live. A **food chain** shows the movement of food energy. Energy moves from one living thing to another. This movement follows a _sequence_. Every food chain starts with producers. Producers such as plants use sunlight to make food. Then animals eat the producers. These animals are then eaten by other animals.

Consumers that are eaten are called **prey**. Consumers that eat prey are called **predators**. In a habitat, some animals are always prey. After prey are eaten by consumers, decomposers break down what remains. They return nutrients to the soil. This helps plants grow.

The acorn is eaten by a chipmunk. Then the hawk eats the chipmunk. ▶

Food Webs

Foods chains may overlap. Food chains that overlap make a **food web**. One kind of producer can be food for different animals. Some consumers eat more than one kind of food.

In an ocean food web, small fish eat producers called *plankton*. The small fish are called *first level consumers*. Then bigger fish eat the small fish. The bigger fish are *second level consumers*. Finally, the biggest fish and mammals eat the bigger fish. They are *top level consumers*.

Complete these Sequence statements.

1. A _____ shows how food chains overlap.

2. _____ are at the start of the ocean food web.

3. Then, _____ consumers, or small fish, eat the plankton.

4. Next, _____ consumers, or middle-sized fish, eat the small fish.

5. Finally, _____ consumers, or the biggest fish and mammals, eat the middle-sized fish.

2.b *Students know* producers and consumers (herbivores, carnivores, omnivores, and decomposers) are related in food chains and food webs and may compete with each other for resources in an ecosystem.

Vocabulary Activity

Healthy Competition

Organisms in the same area need to share food, water, and other resources. They often compete for the resources.

1. The word *habitat* comes from the Latin word *habitare*, meaning "to dwell." What do you think a habitat is?

_____

2. Words can change depending on the *suffix*, or ending. For each word below, write a similar word by changing the suffix.

resources _____

competition _____

VOCABULARY

habitat
resources
competition

How Do Living Things Compete for Resources?

An animal's **habitat** meets its needs.

Animals need **resources** like food, water, and shelter to survive.

© Harcourt

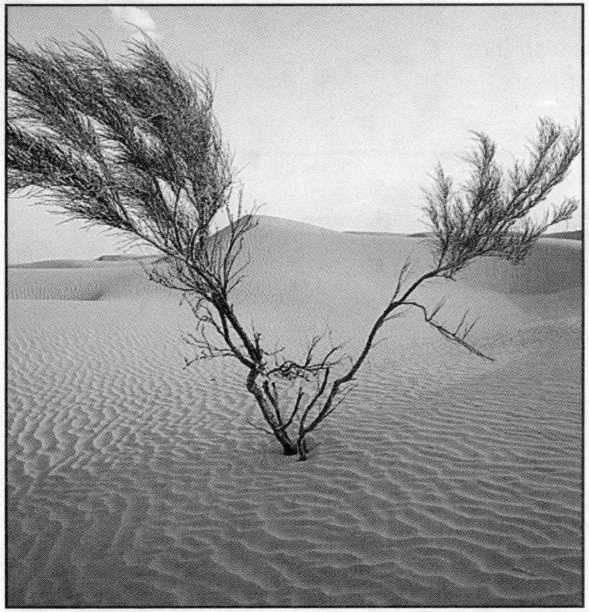

Competition for food is greater when there is less food.

Hands-On Activity
Competing for Resources

You learned how animals compete for food.

1. Draw a picture of some animals that live near your home or school.

2. Draw the food resources that they compete for.

3. Which animal do you think will win? Why?

____

____

____

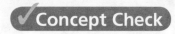

1. A **Cause** is something that makes another thing happen. An **Effect** is the thing that happens. Circle a cause of balance in a habitat. Underline an effect of all the snakes in a habitat dying.

2. What is a habitat?

_____

_____

3. Draw lines to match the habitats to the animals.

Animal	Habitat

Habitats

A **habitat** is a special environment. It meets the needs of a living thing. Habitats can be large or small. An insect is small, so it has a small habitat. A space under a rock can meet the needs of an insect. A bird that migrates needs a larger habitat. That habitat may be an entire continent.

Many types of snakes also live in the desert.

Tarantulas live in the desert.

Each living thing in a habitat has a special *niche* [NITCH]. That means it has a special part to play in its habitat.

All habitats have resources. **Resources** are useful things in the environment. Some resources are food. Others are air, water, and shelter.

Part of a snake's niche is eating mice and birds that live in its habitat. These are the snake's food resources.

If all the snakes in a habitat die, there will be no snakes to eat mice or birds. The numbers of mice and birds will then grow too large. Snakes help keep balance in their habitat. With balance, all three kinds of animals are helped. They all are more likely to survive.

Resources in a desert may be hard to find.

1. What are four resources in a habitat?

_____

_____

_____

_____

2. Complete the cause and effect chart. The first one is done for you.

Cause	Effect
All the snakes in the habitat die	Numbers of mice and birds grow too large
	Habitat stays in balance
Habitat stays in balance	

1. A **Cause** is something that makes another thing happen. An **Effect** is the thing that happens. Circle a cause of competition. Underline an effect of resources being limited.

2. What is the effect of too many of the same kind of animal in a habitat?

_____

3. What resources do plants compete for?

_____

4. Look at the graph below. It shows that as more houses were built near a forest, more birds moved out. What resource were birds competing for?

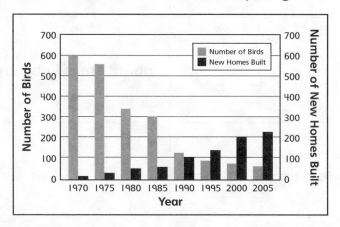

_____

Competing for Resources

In a habitat, resources are limited. There is only a certain amount of food, water, and shelter. No matter how many animals there are, these resources stay the same.

Competition is a kind of contest. Living things compete to win resources. They compete for the things they need to survive. They compete for the same kinds of food. They also compete for shelter.

Leaves are the main food source for deer. Each deer eats a lot of leaves. If there are too many deer, this food will soon be gone.

76

© Harcourt

Plants also compete for space in a habitat. The plants on a rainforest floor are in competition. They compete for the small amount of sun that reaches the forest floor.

A rainforest habitat

Complete these Cause and Effect statements.

1. The right _____ is where animals are able to find food.

2. _____ like food, water, and shelter allow animals to survive better.

3. _____ in a habitat causes the numbers of animals to stay in balance.

4. Because some animals cannot find food, they will not _____.

Unit 2   Review

Circle the letter in front of the best choice.

1. Which comes first in a food chain?

   A producer
   B consumer
   C herbivore
   D carnivore

2. A fish is a food resource. Who would compete for it?

   A consumer and producer
   B omnivore and herbivore
   C carnivore and producer
   D omnivore and carnivore

3. Where do producers get energy to make food?

   A plant matter
   B animal matter
   C sunlight
   D air

4. What is a decomposer's role in an ecosystem?

   A to hunt food
   B to break down wastes
   C to produce food
   D to be hunted

5. Which are NOT decomposers?

   A bacteria
   B mushrooms
   C crows
   D plants

6. What do decomposers do with extra nutrients?

   A Eat them.
   B Store them.
   C Return them to soil.
   D Reuse them at least once.

7. How are omnivores, carnivores, and herbivores related?

   A by food chains and food webs
   B by being from the same place
   C by all being first level consumers
   D by all being second level consumers

8. Consumers that are eaten are called

   A herbivores.
   B carnivores.
   C predators.
   D prey.

Use the picture of a food chain to
answer questions 9 and 10.

9. Which organism is a top level
    consumer?

    A grass
    B flower
    C rabbit
    D owl

10. Which organism is a herbivore?

    A grass
    B flower
    C rabbit
    D owl

11. When do animals compete for
    resources?

    A when they are in the same
    habitat
    B when there are not enough
    C when there are too many
    D when they are in the same
    ecosystem

12. What is a habitat?

    A a special environment
    B a special part an organism
    plays
    C useful thing in the environment
    D a kind of contest

13. A rabbit, a cougar, and grass all
    share a habitat. Order them in a
    food chain.

    _____ _____ _____

14. Explain what a niche is. Give
    an example.

    _____

    _____

    _____

    _____

15. Look back to the question you
    wrote on page 52. Do you have
    an answer for your question? Tell
    what you learned that helps you
    understand how living things get
    energy to survive and grow.

    _____

    _____

    _____

    _____

    _____

    _____

Ecosystems

In this unit, you'll learn all about what makes up an ecosystem, what affects the survival of living things, and the interdependence of living things. What do you know about these topics? What questions do you have?

Thinking Ahead

What do you think an ecosystem is made of? List some parts here.

_____

Draw an example of an animal that uses _camouflage_ in the box below.

Write the name of one kind of microorganism. Then write two things you know about it.

_____

Microorganism

1. _____

2. _____

Write a question you have about ecosystems.

_____

_____

Recording What You Learn

◀ **On this page**, record what you learn as you read the unit.

Lesson 1

For each kind of ecosystem, write one living and one nonliving part.

Ecosystem	Living Part	Nonliving Part
Desert		
Forest		
Ocean		

Lesson 2

Use the space below to draw one example of an adaptation. Then explain how it helps the animal survive in its ecosystem.

Lesson 3

Write one way each pair of living things are dependent on each other.

Ants and aphids _____

_____

Fish and cleaner shrimp _____

_____

Bats and flowers _____

_____

Lesson 4

How are bacteria helpful? How can they be harmful? Give an example of each.

_____

_____

_____

_____

3.a *Students know* ecosystems can be characterized by their living and nonliving components.

Vocabulary Activity

Ecosystems

In this lesson, you'll learn about parts that make up an ecosystem.

1. Fill in the chart. Tell which terms have the prefix.

Prefix	Vocabulary Term (s)
Eco- having to do with the environment	
Bio- having to do with life	

2. *Population* has its roots in a verb. Write the verb here.

_____

VOCABULARY

ecosystem
population
community
biome
ecology

What Makes Up an Ecosystem?

These water birds are part of a pond **ecosystem**.

This **population** of bees lives in a tree.

© Harcourt

This grassland **community** has many populations of animals.

The climate is much the same within this forest **biome**.

By studying **ecology**, we can learn more about ecosystems.

Hands-On Activity
Local Ecosystems

Find out about an ecosystem near you.

1. What kinds of plants live there? Draw one.

2. Name one population of animals that lives there.

3. Give an example of a community within the ecosystem.

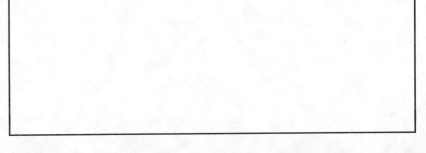

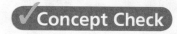

1. The **Main Idea** on these two pages is <u>An ecosystem has in it many living and nonliving things.</u> **Details** tell more about the main idea. Underline two details about an ecosystem.

2. Tell whether each word refers to a nonliving or a living part of an ecosystem, or if it refers to both. Check the correct column.

	Nonliving	**Living**
Populations		
Water		
Individual		
Air		
Part of an ecosystem		

3. How is an individual different from a population?

_____

_____

_____

Individuals and Populations

An **ecosystem** has in it many living and nonliving things. It holds all the things from one *area*, or place. Nonliving things are water, air, sun, and soil. Each living thing is an *individual*. It is just one of its kind.

Individuals of the same kind often live in the same area. This group of individuals is called a **population**.

This individual water lily is part of a population of water lilies.

Many populations make a community in this cold taiga ecosystem.

Communities

A group of populations may live in the same place. This is called a **community**.

There are many communities in Death Valley National Park. This is a very hot, dry place. There are about 1,000 populations of plants here. There are five populations of bats here. There are also three populations of rabbits.

A different place would have different communities. A tidal pool has certain kinds of plants and animals. These animals and plants are not found in a desert.

✓ Concept Check

1. What is a group of populations that live in the same place called?

2. Tell whether each is a community or a population. Put a check in the correct column.

	Community	Population
All the plants in an ecosystem		
All the red squirrels in an ecosystem		
All the coyotes, foxes, and birds in an ecosystem		
A group of tree frogs		
Three kinds of bats in an ecosystem		

3. Where would you find populations of bats, rabbits, and many plants?

4. What determines the kinds of communities you find?

© Harcourt

1. The **Main Idea** on these two pages is <u>Plants and animals need nonliving things to survive.</u> **Details** tell more about the main idea. Underline two details about nonliving things in an ecosystem.

2. List five nonliving parts of an ecosystem.

   1. _____

   2. _____

   3. _____

   4. _____

   5. _____

3. What is a climate made up of?

   _____

   _____

4. Underline the names of two biomes.

Nonliving Parts

Plants and animals need nonliving things to survive. They need water, soil, sunlight, and air. These must be parts of their ecosystem.

Climate includes some nonliving parts of an ecosystem. The amount of sunlight in an ecosystem is one part. The amount of rain is another part. Different patterns of temperature change are another part.

A large area with similar climates and ecosystems is called a **biome**. Deserts and rain forests are biomes.

Water and soil are important nonliving parts of this chipmunk's ecosystem.

Nonliving parts of an ecosystem change. These changes affect the things that live there. A change to very little rain may cause plants to die. Too much rain may cause a flood.

Soil is a nonliving part of an ecosystem. Rich soil helps plants grow.

Sunlight, water, and soil are nonliving parts of an ecosystem. Each part helps plants and animals survive.

✓ Concept Check

1. What nonliving parts of an ecosystem do the living parts need for survival?

   _____

2. What can happen when the nonliving parts of an ecosystem change?

   _____

3. Look at the picture on pages 86 and 87. With a highlighter, color all the nonliving parts. Circle all of the animals.

1. The **Main Idea** on these two pages is <u>Ecosystems have their own living and nonliving parts.</u> **Details** tell more about the main idea. Underline one detail about the living parts of a desert ecosystem, and one detail about the nonliving parts.

2. What is the study of ecosystems called?

_____

3. Fill in the chart about the desert ecosystem. Put the parts in the correct columns.

Nonliving Parts	Living Parts

4. Look at the pictures. Name two ecosystems other than a desert.

_____

Ecosystems

Each **ecosystem** has its own living and nonliving parts. A desert ecosystem has cactus plants. It has spiders and lots of sunlight. It has very little rain. A forest ecosystem has different plants and animals. It has different amounts of rain and sun.

An ecosystem can be large, like a desert. It can be small, like the space under a rock. Each ecosystem has living and nonliving parts. Each has climate. The climate may be cool and wet. It may be warm and dry.

Prairie dogs live in a grassland.

Ecology is the study of ecosystems. Ecologists study the living and nonliving parts of an ecosystem. They look at how these parts affect one another. They look at how plants help animals. They look at how animals help plants. They look at ways living things depend on nonliving things in an ecosystem.

Moose survive well in a forest ecosystem.

Complete this Main Idea statement.

1. An _____ is an area and every living and nonliving thing in it.

Complete these Detail statements.

2. A _____ is a group of the same kind of thing living in one place.

3. Populations of different things in the same place make a _____.

4. Two examples of a _____ are a rain forest and a desert.

3.b *Students know* ecosystems can be characterized by their living and nonliving components.

Vocabulary Activity

Adapting and Accommodating

In this lesson, you'll learn how animals and plants are suited to their environment. Some have special features that help them survive.

1. The verb *adapt* means "to change in order to fit." What is the suffix in the word *adaptation*?

_____

2. The word *accommodation* has the same suffix. What root is it attached to?

_____

VOCABULARY

adaptation
accommodation

What Affects Survival?

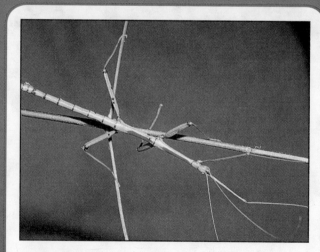

This insect's body parts are an **adaptation**. The insect blends in to look like part of a tree.

Hands-On Activity
Ocean Adaptations

1. Draw an ocean ecosystem in the space below. Include some animals and plants in the picture.

2. Write one adaptation of each of the animals and plants you drew.

Plant or Animal	Adaptation

3. Choose one of the adaptations you wrote above. Explain how it works.

_____

_____

_____

People make **accommodations** in cold weather. They wear different clothes to stay warm.

1. The **Main Idea** on these two pages is <u>Plants and animals must adapt or accommodate or die.</u> **Details** tell more about the main idea. Underline one detail about adaptation and one detail about accommodation.

2. What must plants and animals adapt to?

_____

3. Look at the picture. How is the hummingbird's beak an adaptation?

_____

_____

4. Fill in the map. Show the options available to an animal or plant when an ecosystem changes.

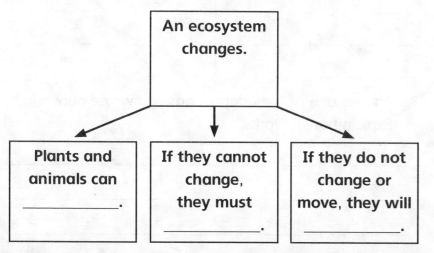

An ecosystem changes.

| Plants and animals can _____. | If they cannot change, they must _____. | If they do not change or move, they will _____. |

Adaptation and Accommodation

Ecosystems change. They become hotter and drier. They become cooler or wetter. The plants and animals that live there must change, too. If they cannot change, they must move to a new place. If not, they will die.

An adaptation is a body part or behavior. **Adaptations** help living things survive in a particular ecosystem. Heavy fur is an adaptation. It protects a bear from the cold.

A hummingbird's beak is an adaptation. It helps the bird reach into a flower for food.

If bears' habitats are taken away to build homes, bears will look for food near homes.

Adaptations are also behaviors. Some animals migrate in winter. They go where it is warmer. Some animals *hibernate*. They sleep all winter. Animals are born knowing how to do these things.

Other times, animals learn new things to survive. Some animals have learned new ways to get food. Some bears go to places where people are. They find food that people leave behind. This change in behavior is an **accommodation**. It helps the bears survive.

In California, bears getting food from trash cans is a problem.

✓ Concept Check

1. Name an adaptation.

_____

2. How is an adaptation different from an accommodation?

_____

_____

3. How is an adaptation like an accommodation?

_____

_____

4. Fill in the chart about animal behaviors. Check the correct column to tell if it is an adaptation or an accommodation.

	Adaptation	Accommodation
Migrating		
Bears looking for food in the trash		
Hibernating		
Squirrels taking food from people		

1. The **Main Idea** on these two pages is <u>Rainforest organisms have their own adaptations.</u> **Details** tell more about the main idea. Underline two details about adaptations that help plants and animals survive in the rain forest.

2. Name two adaptations of rain forest plants.

_____

_____

3. Draw a picture of a tall rain forest tree and a small rain forest plant. Your picture should show the small plant's adaptations.

```



```

Tropical Rain Forests

In a rain forest, tall trees block the sun from plants below. Little sun reaches plants on the ground. Many plants near the ground have large leaves. This helps them get as much sun as possible. Without large leaves, these plants would not grow well. They might die.

Some rain forest plants have vines. This helps them reach sunlight. Other leaves have grooves. These help rain water run off quickly. Otherwise, too much rain could break them.

An orchid's roots are an adaptation. They let the orchid grow on high branches. Then it can get more sun.

This bird's beak is an adaptation. It helps the bird get food from the ends of tree branches.

Camouflage [KAM•uh•flazh] helps some animals hide. They have a color or shape that helps them look like their surroundings. Many rain forest lizards are green. Their color helps them blend in. This makes it harder for predators to find them.

Camouflage also helps some predators. Snakes in a rain forest blend in with vines and leaves. They can get close to prey and not be seen. Then it is easier for them to catch food.

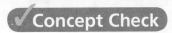 **Concept Check**

1. How does camouflage help some animals in the rain forest survive?

_____

2. Give an example of camouflage.

_____

3. Fill in the chart. Tell how each adaptation helps plants or animals survive in their rain forest ecosystem.

Adaptation	How Is It Helpful?
Large leaves	
Vines	
Grooves in leaves	
Predator's camouflage	
Prey's camouflage	

1. The **Main Idea** on these two pages is <u>Coral reef organisms have their own adaptations.</u> **Details** tell more about the main idea. Underline two details about adaptations of plants and animals in the coral reef.

2. What are coral reefs?

_____

3. What do many coral reef animals have that helps them hide?

_____

4. Draw a coral reef animal. Write a sentence about its adaptation.

Animal	Adaptation
	_____
	_____
	_____
	_____
	_____

Coral Reefs

Coral reefs are living things. They are made of many small organisms. Populations of hundreds of living things live on or around reefs. The plants and animals that live on coral reefs have made adaptations. These adaptations help them survive on the reef. Many animals on coral reefs have camouflage. Their color helps them hide.

Small reef fish swim in *schools*, or large groups. This adaptation protects the small fish. A predator doesn't know which fish to hunt.

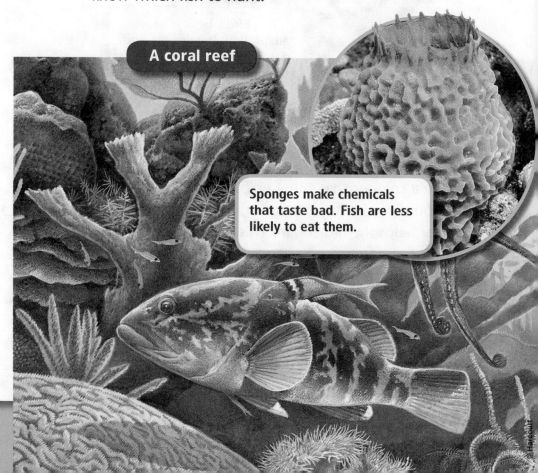

A coral reef

Sponges make chemicals that taste bad. Fish are less likely to eat them.

Coral is also adapted to its environment. A coral reef is made of many tiny coral animals. Coral cannot move around. They eat plankton when it comes by them in the water.

Coral also need algae to survive. Algae inside the coral help feed them. Algae share food with the coral. The coral give the algae a home. The coral also give off carbon dioxide. The algae need this to make food.

A clownfish lives with anemones. Their sting helps keep predators away.

This crab uses seaweed and small shells as camouflage.

1. What adaptation in behavior helps small fish in a coral reef survive?

_____

2. Fill in the chart. Tell how each adaptation helps plants or animals survive in their coral reef ecosystem.

Adaptation	How Is It Helpful?
Camouflage	
Clownfish living with anemones	
Coral letting algae live inside it	
Making chemicals that taste bad	

3. Name an adaptation from these two pages that is **NOT** a behavior.

_____

4. Name an adaptation from these two pages that **IS** a behavior.

_____

1. The **Main Idea** on these two pages is <u>Desert organisms have their own adaptations.</u> **Details** tell more about the main idea. Underline two details about adaptations of plants and animals in the desert ecosystem.

2. What kinds of adaptations help desert plants live?

_____

3. What kinds of adaptations help desert animals live?

_____

4. Fill in the chart. Tell how each adaptation helps plants or animals survive in their desert ecosystem.

Adaptation	How Is It Helpful?
Light brown color	
Spines	
Sleeping under the ground	
Hunting at night	

Deserts

It is hard for plants and animals to survive in a desert. In a desert, many animals use camouflage. Light brown colors help animals hide. Light colors also help keep them cool.

Many desert animals stay out of the sun. When temperatures are highest, they sleep. Many sleep in the daytime. Some sleep under rocks. Others sleep in burrows under the ground. At night, the air is cooler. Then these animals come out and hunt for food.

A desert ecosystem has many plants and animals. Adaptations help them survive in the hot, dry climate.

Most desert plants have spines. Having spines, not leaves, helps desert plants save water. Spines also keep animals from eating the plants.

Another adaptation helps cactus plants. They have roots that are close to the top of the ground. The roots can take in rain water quickly.

This bird nests in a cactus. The cactus spines keep predators away.

Complete this Main Idea statement.

1. When _____ change, the plants and animals in them will change, move, or die.

Complete these Detail statements.

2. Animals with adaptations for a rain forest probably would not survive in a_____.

3. _____ help living things survive in a particular ecosystem.

4. Some animals use _____ to hide.

3.c *Students know* many plants depend on animals for pollination and seed dispersal, and animals depend on plants for food and shelter.

Vocabulary Activity

Interdependence

In an ecosystem, animals and plants depend on each other. Sometimes they need help to survive.

1. You have heard the word *relationship* used before. Write a definition for it.

_____

2. These vocabulary words have been broken into parts. The parts have been defined. Put them back together, and write what you think the vocabulary word means.

Vocabulary Word	Broken Down	Meaning
Interdependence	*Inter-* = between two or more *dependence* = relying on another	
Pollinate	*Pollin* = from *pollen*, a powder that helps make seeds *-ate* = to apply something	

Lesson **3**

What Is Interdependence?

VOCABULARY
interdependence
pollinate
relationship

There is **interdependence** between flowers and bees.

When bees eat nectar, they also **pollinate** the flowers.

Hands-On Activity
Interdependent Animals Poster

1. Find or draw pictures of three pairs of plants or animals that help each other.

2. On a large piece of paper, glue or tape the pictures in two columns, leaving an empty column down the middle.

3. In the space between each pair, write a sentence that tells how they help each other.

Your finished poster should look like this:

Predators have a **relationship** with their prey.

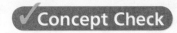

✓ Concept Check

1. You **Compare** when you look at how things are alike. You **Contrast** when you look at how things are different. Compare fish and cleaner shrimp to ants and aphids.

	Same	Different
Fish and cleaner shimp		
Ants and aphids		

2. What is interdependence?

_____

3. Why do living things depend on each other?

_____

4. Two animals do not compete for food. They help each other. Circle the word that tells what they have.

Interdependence

Interdependence means that things depend on each other. Two living things may depend on each other for survival.

Groups of living things may be interdependent. Elephants live in herds. They help protect each other. They survive better in groups.

Sometimes different kinds of animals help each other. They do not compete for food. They have a special connection. They have a **relationship**.

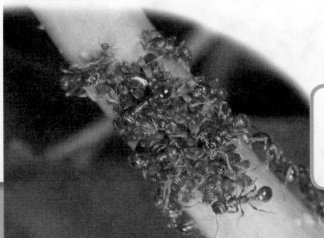

Ants help aphids by taking them to their nest at night. This keeps the aphids safe. Aphids give food to the ants.

This clownfish lives with anemones in a coral reef. The two are interdependent.

1. Compare the relationships between shrimp and fish and between elephants in a group.

_____

2. Draw lines between the names of the organisms to show which have a relationship.

ants	**fish**
anemone	**elephants**
other elephants	**clownfish**
shrimp	**aphids**

3. Who benefits from the relationship between cleaner shrimp and fish?

_____

Cleaner shrimp have a relationship with fish. The fish have harmful organisms living on them. These *parasites* can hurt the fish. But cleaner shrimp eat the parasites. This helps the fish. It also gives food to the shrimp.

The shrimp and fish are *interdependent*. They help each other survive.

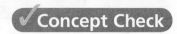

✓ Concept Check

1. You **Compare** when you look at how things are alike. You **Contrast** when you look at how things are different. Put check marks in this chart to compare pollinators and seed-eaters.

	Pollinators	Seed-Eaters
Help plants		
Drop seeds as waste in new places		
Carry pollen from one flower to another		

2. Draw a plant with an adaptation that keeps it from being eaten.

Animals Help Plants

Animals help plants in two ways. Some **pollinate** the flowers of plants. They carry pollen from one flower to another. Birds and other small animals do this as they feed themselves.

Seeds are also eaten by birds and other animals. Then later these animals drop the seeds as waste. New plants can grow in new places. Dogs, cats, and bears may carry seeds from one place to the next. They carry the seeds on their fur.

Fruit bats carry pollen between flowers. ▶

◀ Dogs carry seeds that get stuck in their fur.

Plants Help Animals

All animals need plants. Herbivores eat plants. Then carnivores eat herbivores. Plants also protect animals from predators.

Plants help people, too. People use wood from trees to make paper and fuel. Coal that comes from decayed plants can be used to make electricity. Cotton for clothes comes from plants. People use some plants for medicines.

Thorns help keep predators from eating these plants.

Complete these compare and contrast statements.

1. Plants and animals are alike in that they need each other to _____.

2. Some shrimp help keep fish clean. The fish gives _____ to the shrimp.

3. Pollen and seeds both get carried away by _____.

4. Both dogs and birds take seeds away. This helps _____ grow in new places.

3.d *Students know* many plants depend on animals for pollination and seed dispersal, and animals depend on plants for food and shelter.

Vocabulary Activity

Microorganisms

You already learned what a microorganism is. Now you'll learn about different kinds that are common in our world.

1. Below is a table of root words and their meanings. Write how you think each vocabulary word got its name.

Vocabulary Word	Root meaning	Why named?
Bacteria	*Rod-shaped*	
Mold	*Smallest measure*	
Protist	*Former kingdom name, meaning "the very first."*	

2. The prefix *micro-* means "tiny." The suffix *–scope* means "to look at." What do you think a microscope helps you do?

_____

Lesson **4**

What Are Microorganisms?

VOCABULARY

microscope
bacteria
mold
protist

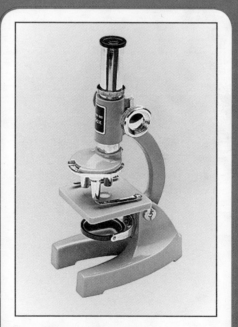
This **microscope** makes very tiny things look larger.

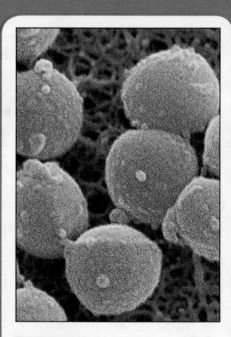
Bacteria can be seen only with a microscope.

© Harcourt

Mold is growing on this bread.

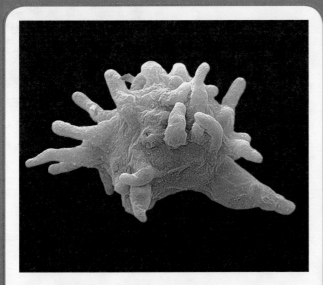

This **protist** is a kind of microorganism.

Hands-On Activity
Helpful and Harmful Bacteria

1. Research different kinds of bacteria. Look online, in magazines, or in newspapers. Find at least four kinds.

2. Draw, print out, or cut out a picture of each kind of bacteria you chose. Glue or tape the pictures to a piece of posterboard.

3. For each kind of bacteria, write one helpful thing or one harmful thing it does. Your poster should show at least one helpful thing.

4. Talk about your poster in class. Did anyone else choose the same bacteria? If so, did he or she find out something different about it? Describe any new information.

_____

_____

_____

_____

_____

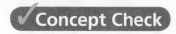
1. Protists can be like plants and animals. Give an example of each kind of protist.

	Like Plants	Like Animals
Protists	Some can make their own food.	Some must hunt for food.
	_____	_____

2. List four ways microorganisms help people and animals.

1. _____

2. _____

3. _____

4. _____

Kinds of Microorganisms

Bacteria are very tiny. They can only be seen under a **microscope**. Bacteria are microorganisms. Yeasts and molds are microorganisms. They are also fungi. They cannot make their own food.

Protists are a special kind of microorganism. Some protists, like *algae*, can make their own food. In this way, algae are like plants. Other protists, like *protozoans*, hunt for food. In this way, protozoans are like animals.

Some microorganisms are harmful. Some bacteria in raw meat or eggs can make people sick. Cooking kills the bacteria and makes the food safe.

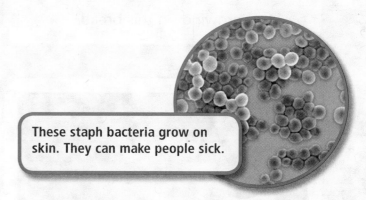

These staph bacteria grow on skin. They can make people sick.

Helpful Microorganisms

Microorganisms help people more than harm them. *Plankton* in the ocean put oxygen into the air. They are also food for fish.

Other microorganisms are used to clean up waste water. They get rid of harmful bacteria in the water. Microorganisms also help clean up oil spills.

Bacteria turn milk into yogurt. They help make some cheeses. The bacteria *penicillin* is made into medicine.

Yeast feeds on sugar in bread dough. It makes bread rise.

Complete these Compare and Contrast statements.

1. Bacteria and other microorganisms can be seen only under a _____.

2. Yeasts and molds are both microorganisms and _____.

3. _____ can act like plants or animals.

4. _____ help people more than harm them.

Circle the letter in front of the best choice.

1. In which answer choice are the words arranged from *smallest* to *largest*?

   A habitat   biome   ecosystem

   B ecosystem   biome   habitat

   C habitat   ecosystem   biome

   D biome   ecosystem   habitat

2. All of the koala bears in an area make up

   A a population.

   B an ecosystem.

   C a community.

   D an individuals.

3. Which is a nonliving thing that animals and plants in an ecosystem need to survive?

   A biome

   B water

   C ecology

   D decomposer

4. Any body part or behavior that helps a plant or animal survive in its ecosystem is called

   A a migration.

   B a camouflage.

   C an accommodation.

   D an adaptation.

5. This tiger is camouflaged by grass. How does this adaptation help it survive its environment?

   A It keeps predators away.

   B It hides it from prey.

   C It keeps it cool during the day.

   D It helps it survive cold winters.

6. A new plant was brought to the tropical rain forest. It has small leaves and grows low to the ground. How will it survive?

   A It will not. It has no adaptations for getting sunlight.

   B It will begin to grow bigger and bigger leaves.

   C It will climb on vines to reach the sun.

   D It will not. It takes in too much water.

7. Which adaptation helps desert plants keep animals from eating them?

   A roots close to the top of the ground

   B thick stems

   C light brown color

   D spines

8. Ants bring aphids to their nest. Aphids give ants food. What kind of relationship is this?

A predator-prey

B interdependence

C producer-consumer

D competition

Use the picture to answer question 9.

9. How is the bee helping the flower?

A by eating seeds

B by bringing it food

C by carrying pollen

D by carrying seeds

10. Which is NOT a reason animals (including people) need plants?

A for protection from predators

B for food

C for medicine

D for car engines

11. Which is NOT an example of a microorganism?

A bacteria

B protists

C mushrooms

D plankton

12. Which is NOT something microorganisms can do?

A be made into medicine

B put oxygen in the air

C clean up waste water

D make new energy

13. How is coral adapted to its environment? Explain.

_____

_____

_____

_____

_____

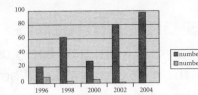

14. The chart shows the rabbit and wolf populations in an ecosystem. Why does the number of rabbits increase as the number of wolves decreases?

_____

_____

_____

_____

15. Look back at the question you wrote on page 81. Do you have an answer for your question? Tell what you learned that helps you understand ecosystems.

_____

_____

_____

_____

Rocks and Minerals

In this unit, you'll learn how rocks and minerals are identified and how the rock cycle works. What do you know about these topics? What questions do you have?

💭 Thinking Ahead

Think of a mineral you know. Draw some of its properties, such as color and texture.

What are some different kinds of rock? Write three of your ideas.

_____

_____

_____

Draw a picture that shows how you think rocks are made.

Write a question you have about rocks and minerals.

_____

_____

_____

Recording What You Learn

◄ **On this page, record what you learn as you read the unit.**

Lesson 1

What are the six properties of a mineral?

1. _____   2. _____   3. _____

4. _____   5. _____   6. _____

Lesson 2

Tell how each kind of rock is formed.

igneous _____

sedimentary _____

metamorphic _____

What are two properties of rocks?

_____

Lesson 3

Draw the rock cycle in the box below. You may use the picture on page 133 to help.

4.b *Students know* how to identify common rock-forming minerals (including quartz, calcite, feldspar, mica, and hornblende) and ore minerals by using a table of diagnostic properties.

Vocabulary Activity

Mineral Identification

Did you ever see an interesting rock and wonder what it was? In this lesson, you'll learn how minerals are identified. Minerals help make up rocks.

I. The term *mineral* comes from the Latin word *mineralis*, which is the word for a mine. Why do you think minerals got their name?

2. The other vocabulary terms are adjectives. As you read the lesson, fill in the chart to show what the terms describe.

Term	Describes
Streak	
Luster	
Cleavage	
Fracture	
Hardness	

Lesson **1**

How Are Minerals Identified?

VOCABULARY

mineral
streak
luster
cleavage
fracture
hardness

I found a **mineral** while I was hiking in the woods.

I rub the mineral on a white tile. The **streak** it leaves is brown-colored.

My mineral has a metallic **luster**. It looks shiny, like a metal.

My mineral has **cleavage**. It will break into pieces that are flat.

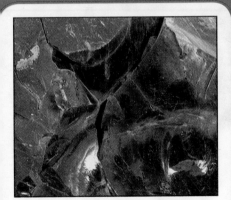

My mineral will **fracture** when I hit it with a hammer. The pieces break off in curved clumps.

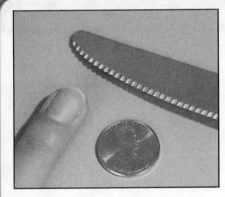

My mineral has a low **hardness**. It is not hard. I can scratch it with my fingernail.

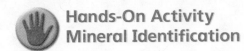

Hands-On Activity
Mineral Identification

Compare the colors and streak properties of two minerals.

My minerals: _____

1. Describe the color of each mineral.

_____

2. How does each mineral's streak compare with its color?

_____

3. Why isn't color a good way to identify minerals?

_____

_____

1. The **Main Idea** on these two pages is <u>A mineral is a natural solid that was never living.</u> **Details** tell more about the main idea. Underline two details about minerals.

2. Name three things that form a mineral.

   1. _____

   2. _____

   3. _____

3. Fill in the blanks in the sequence boxes. Tell how a diamond forms.

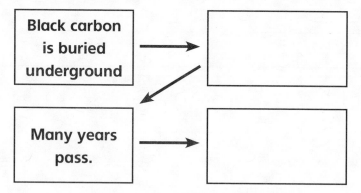

Black carbon is buried underground	
Many years pass.	

Minerals and How They Form

What exactly is a mineral? A **mineral** is a natural solid that was never living. Minerals are not rocks. Some minerals are formed deep inside Earth. Minerals are formed by pressure, temperature, and time.

Have you ever seen a diamond? A diamond begins as black carbon buried deep underground. The ground presses down on the carbon. After many, many years, the carbon changes into a hard diamond. A diamond is a mineral.

Other mineral crystals also form deep inside Earth. Melted rock, or magma, cools and forms the mineral crystals.

California's state gem, benitoite [buh•NEE•toh•yt]

116

Amethyst is a type of the mineral quartz.

Minerals also form inside geodes (JEE•ohdz). Geodes are often round. They usually look dull on the outside. The inside of a geode has crystals that may be brightly colored. A geode may begin as a hole in mud or sand. In time, the hole fills with water and dissolved minerals. After time, the water evaporates. The minerals are left as crystals inside the geode.

Not all minerals form inside Earth. Some form inside caves from dripping water. After the water evaporates, mineral deposits are left behind.

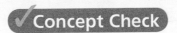

1. Look at the picture on page 116. How did California's state mineral form?

_____

_____

2. Fill in the chart to tell what a geode looks like.

Inside	Outside

3. Number the steps to show how a geode forms.

_____ There is a hole in mud or sand.

_____ Minerals are left as crystals inside the geode.

_____ The water evaporates.

_____ The hole fills with water and dissolved minerals.

1. The **Main Idea** on these two pages is <u>Color and streak are two properties that can be used to identify minerals.</u> **Details** tell more about the main idea. Underline two details about how color and streak can be used to identify minerals.

2. How many minerals have scientists discovered?

   _____

3. Look at the picture. Name five colors of quartz.

   _____

4. Two colors of quartz have names that don't use the word "quartz." Circle them.

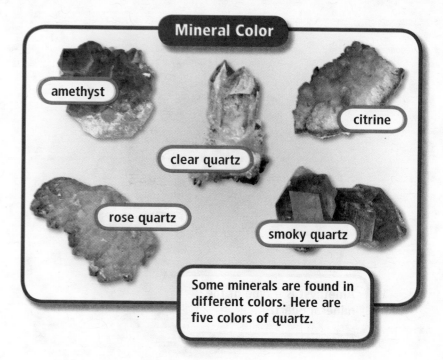

Mineral Color

amethyst

clear quartz

citrine

rose quartz

smoky quartz

Some minerals are found in different colors. Here are five colors of quartz.

Color and Streak

Quartz, rubies, diamonds, and salt are types of minerals. Scientists have found 3000 different minerals on Earth! How can we identify all the different minerals?

Minerals have properties. A *property* is a special feature you can identify. Some minerals are hard, and some are soft. Some have color, and some are clear.

Pure quartz is a clear mineral. Sometimes the quartz will have other materials inside it. These materials can change the color of quartz. Quartz can be pink, purple, gray, or orange.

Some minerals can change color in other ways. Pyrite is a mineral that looks like gold. It will turn black when air and rain touch it for a long time.

You cannot always identify a mineral by its color. Sometimes you must study other properties, such as its streak. When a mineral is rubbed against something hard, a powder is left. The color of the powder is called **streak**. A streak plate is a rough white tile. You can rub a mineral on a streak plate to see the colored powder.

Often the streak is the same color as the mineral. Sometimes the mineral and streak do not match. A mineral's streak will always have the same color, even if the mineral has different colors. Hematite is a mineral with many colors. It can be black, dark brown, or silvery. However, hematite always leaves a reddish brown streak.

You learned about two properties of minerals: *color* and *streak*. You can use color or streak to identify a mineral. Testing the streak is usually better than seeing the color.

How can we identify minerals?

Mineral Streak

These two pieces of hematite are different colors, but their streaks are the same. ▼

▲ Sulfur, magnetite, hematite, and galena all have different streaks.

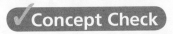

1. In the box below, draw a student conducting a streak test. Label the parts of the test.

2. Use the picture and the text to fill in the chart. Choose two minerals. Write their names. Tell their streak color.

Mineral	Streak Color

3. Why is streak a better property than color for identifying minerals?

_____

_____

119

© Harcourt

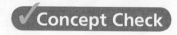

Concept Check

1. The **Main Idea** on these two pages is <u>Luster, cleavage, and fracture can be used to identify minerals.</u> **Details** tell about the main idea. Underline two details about luster, cleavage, or fracture.

2. Look at the picture. Fill in the chart by describing each mineral's luster.

Mineral	Luster
Kaolinite	
Pyrite	
Topaz	
Gypsum	
Artinite	
Talc	
Wulfenite	

Luster, Cleavage, and Fracture

Minerals can reflect light. The way the light reflects is called **luster**. Luster is another property of minerals.

Many minerals shine like metal. They have a *metallic* luster. Have you seen light reflecting off a shiny silver pan? That kind of a shine is a metallic luster.

Some minerals do not shine like metal. They have a *nonmetallic* luster. They have glassy, silky, waxy, pearly, earthy, resinous, or greasy luster.

Mineral Luster

▲ Kaolinite (KAY•uh•luh•nyt) has an earthy luster.

▲ Gypsum (JIP•suhm) has a glassy, silky, or pearly luster.

▲ Pyrite (PY•ryt) has a metallic luster.

▲ Wulfenite (WUL•fuh•nyt) has a resinous or greasy luster.

▲ Talc has a greasy luster.

▲ Artinite (AR•tin•yt) has a shiny luster.

▲ Topaz (TOH•paz) has a glassy luster.

Mineral Cleavage and Fracture

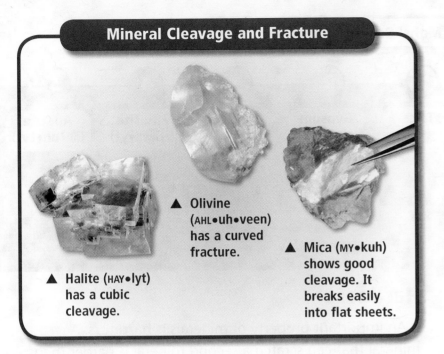

▲ Olivine (AHL•uh•veen) has a curved fracture.

▲ Halite (HAY•lyt) has a cubic cleavage.

▲ Mica (MY•kuh) shows good cleavage. It breaks easily into flat sheets.

The way a mineral breaks is another property we can study. Minerals break apart in different ways. A mineral that splits along a smooth, flat surface has **cleavage**. Diamond is one kind of mineral that has cleavage. A diamond will always break along a flat surface.

Some minerals do not break along a flat surface. Instead, they **fracture**. Fracture is another property of minerals. Fractured minerals will look like rough clumps or curved pieces. Quartz fractures to form curved pieces. Talc fractures to form rough clumps.

Some minerals can do both. They have both fracture and cleavage when they break.

✓ **Concept Check**

1. What are two ways minerals break?

_____

_____

2. Describe what it means to say that a mineral fractures.

_____

3. Look at the pictures and the text on this page. Sort all of the minerals by whether they fracture or have cleavage.

Fracture	Have Cleavage

✓ Concept Check

1. The **Main Idea** on these two pages is <u>An important property of minerals is hardness.</u> **Details** tell more about the main idea. Underline two details about hardness.

2. Look at the Mohs Hardness Scale. Use it to put the minerals in the chart in order. Number them 1-10, with one being the softest mineral.

Mineral	Order
Orthoclase	
Fluorite	
Gypsum	
Ruby	
Calcite	
Diamond	
Apatite	
Quartz	
Talc	
Topaz	

3. Can calcite scratch ruby? How do you know?

_____

4. What mineral can scratch a diamond?

_____

Mohs' Scale of Mineral Hardness

1	2	3	4	5
Talc	Gypsum	Calcite	Fluorite (FLAWR•yt)	Apatite (AP•uh•tyt)

Hardness

An important property of minerals is **hardness**. A mineral that can scratch a second mineral is harder than the second mineral. The second mineral is softer than the first mineral.

Minerals are measured from 1 to 10 on a scale called the *Mohs' hardness scale*. Talc is the softest mineral, so it is ranked 1. Diamond is the hardest mineral, so it is ranked 10. A diamond can scratch all other minerals. It can even scratch another diamond. A mineral can scratch any mineral with a hardness lower than or the same as its own hardness.

Look at the scale on these pages. Fluorite (FLAWR•yt) is ranked 4. Apatite is ranked 5. That means that apatite is harder than fluorite.

6	7	8	9	10
Orthoclase	Quartz	Topaz	Ruby	Diamond

If you find a mineral, use the Mohs' scale to help you find out the hardness of your mineral. What minerals can it scratch? What can scratch your mineral?

Complete this Main Idea statement.

1. A _____ can be identified by studying its properties.

Complete these Detail statements.

2. Minerals leave a colored powder called _____ when they are rubbed on a rough tile.

3. The property of how light reflects off a mineral's surface is called _____.

4. If a mineral splits along a smooth, flat surface, it has _____.

California Standards in This Lesson

 4.C *Students know* how to differentiate among igneous, sedimentary, and metamorphic rocks by referring to their properties and methods of formation (the rock cycle).

Vocabulary Activity

Rocks

Just as minerals can be identified, so, too, can rocks.

I. Sedimentary, igneous, and metamorphic are all kinds of rocks. The chart below shows the roots of their names. How do you think the rocks formed?

Vocabulary Term	Meaning of Root Word	How Formed
Igneous rock	*Ignis:* = fire	
Sedimentary	*Sediment:* small pieces of rock	
Metamorphic	*Morph:* to change	

Lesson 2

How Are Rocks Identified?

VOCABULARY

rock
igneous rock
sedimentary rock
metamorphic rock

I found a **rock** while I was on vacation. It is very hard, and it has layers.

© Harcourt

Granite is a beautiful type of **igneous** rock.

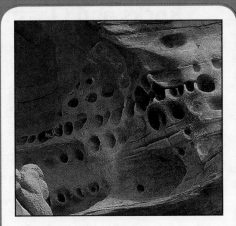

You can see many **sedimentary rocks** at the Grand Canyon.

Metamorphic rock, such as gneiss, is formed due to high temperature and pressure.

Hands-On Activity
Finding Calcite

If vinegar is poured on the mineral calcite, bubbles will appear. Choose three rocks. Place a few drops of vinegar on each rock.

1. Do your rocks contain the mineral calcite? How do you know?

_____

_____

2. Compare and contrast the rocks.

_____

_____

_____

_____

_____

_____

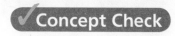

Concept Check

1. You **Compare** when you look at how things are alike. You **Contrast** when you look at how things are different. Compare granite and diorite.

Rocks	Same	Different
Granite and Diorite		

2. What are the two types of textures that help you classify rocks?

_____

_____

3. What is a rock made of?

_____

4. You can see pieces in coarse-grain textured rocks. What are you seeing?

_____

Rocks and Classification

Rocks are made up of one or more minerals. Most rocks are mineral mixtures. You can identify types of rock by the different minerals inside them.

A rock has *texture*. Texture is a property you can use to classify rocks. Some rocks have a small-grained texture. The minerals are in tiny pieces, like very fine sand. Some rocks have a coarse-grained texture. You can see the different minerals easily with your eye.

These rocks are alike. They both have the same minerals. The rocks are also different. They have different *amounts* of the minerals.

granite

diorite

Igneous Rock

There are three big groups of rock. The groups are based on how the rocks form.

Igneous rock forms when melted rock cools and hardens. Igneous rock can form underground or on Earth's surface.

How igneous rocks look depends on where they formed. Igneous rocks that form underground usually have large crystals inside them. This is because melted rock cools more slowly underground. When melted rock cools slowly, mineral crystals have time to grow.

When melted rock cools quickly, it hardens before mineral crystals can grow large. Igneous rocks that form on Earth's surface have small crystals. Some even have no crystals at all.

granite

Granite, diorite, and gabbro all form underneath Earth's surface. They have large mineral crystals.

diorite (DY•uh•ryt)

gabbro (GAB•roh)

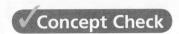
1. What is igneous rock?

_____

_____

2. In what two ways can igneous rocks look different from one another?

_____

3. Fill in the chart. Tell whether the crystals will be large or small, based on how the rock formed.

How Igneous Rock Formed	Crystals Will Be
Slowly	
Above-ground	
Quickly	
Underground	

1. You **Compare** when you look at how things are alike. You **Contrast** when you look at how things are different. Compare sandstone and coal.

_____

Contrast sandstone and coal.

_____

_____

2. Fill in the chart. Tell how seasonal weather changes rock into sediment.

Season	Action
Winter	
Spring	
Summer	
Fall	

3. What are little pieces of broken-off rock called?

_____

Sedimentary Rock

Imagine a rock at the top of a mountain. Every spring, rain falls on the rock. The rain dissolves some of the rock's minerals. In the summer, heat makes the rock crack. Small pieces flake off. Autumn comes. The wind blows dust against the rock. The dust scratches the rock's surface. In the winter, water seeps into cracks in the rock. The water freezes. Freezing water expands. This breaks off more pieces of rock.

The rock is slowly being worn away. What happens to all the little pieces of rock that have broken off? The pieces are called _sediment_.

Types of Sedimentary Rocks

▲ Sandstone has pieces of sediment the size of grains of sand.

▲ Limestone usually forms in oceans. It has parts of shells in it.

▲ Chert has a lot of silica in it. It often forms on the ocean floor.

▲ Coal forms from the remains of plants.

Many sedimentary rocks, such as this shale, begin as sediment layers on the bottom of a river.

Water and wind carry away the sediment. Then the sediment collects in other places.

Over time, sediment piles up. One layer builds up on top of another. The top layers push down on the bottom layers. The water is pressed out. If the water contained minerals, the minerals may be left behind. They may act like cement. The cement makes the pieces of sediment stick together.

Sedimentary rock has layers of sediment that are stuck together. Because of the way it is formed, sedimentary rock is often softer than other types of rock.

✓ Concept Check

1. What is a sedimentary rock?

_____

2. Compare and contrast limestone and chert.

Rocks	Alike	Different
Limestone and Chert		

3. What acts like cement to make pieces of sediment stick together?

_____

4. Why is sedimentary rock softer than other types of rock?

_____

1. You **Compare** when you look at how things are alike. You **Contrast** when you look at how things are different. Compare schist and slate.

_____

_____

2. What is needed for any kind of rock to become metamorphic?

_____

_____

3. Describe how rocks form deep inside Earth.

_____

_____

4. Look at pages 127–131. Fill in the chart to show how each rock forms.

Rock Classification	How Rock Forms
Igneous	
Sedimentary	
Metamorphic	

Metamorphic Rock

It is very hot deep inside Earth. The high temperature makes the rock inside Earth soft. The weight of everything on top of the rock squashes it. The rock flattens and becomes more dense, or solid. It may form layers.

If the temperature and pressure are very high, rock that does not melt can still change and become **metamorphic rock**.

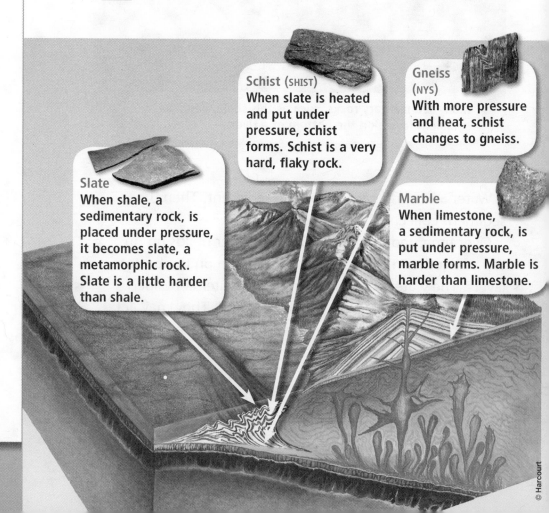

Schist (SHIST)
When slate is heated and put under pressure, schist forms. Schist is a very hard, flaky rock.

Gneiss (NYS)
With more pressure and heat, schist changes to gneiss.

Slate
When shale, a sedimentary rock, is placed under pressure, it becomes slate, a metamorphic rock. Slate is a little harder than shale.

Marble
When limestone, a sedimentary rock, is put under pressure, marble forms. Marble is harder than limestone.

Metamorphic rock can also form under the ocean and near volcanoes.

With enough pressure and high enough temperature, sedimentary rock and igneous rock can change. They can become metamorphic rock. Metamorphic rocks are very hard. Many have mineral crystals that are arranged in stripes. High temperature makes crystals become soft. Then high pressure locks them together. Sometimes the crystals flow into stripes.

Complete these Compare and Contrast statements.

1. The _____ of a fine-grained rock is different from that of a coarse-grained rock.

2. Metamorphic rock forms with extreme heat and pressure. _____ rock forms when rocks are melted and then cooled.

3. _____ rock is usually softer than igneous rock.

4. Igneous rocks formed underground have _____ and _____ crystals than igneous rocks formed above ground.

California Standards in This Lesson

 4.c *Students know* how to differentiate among igneous, sedimentary, and metamorphic rocks by referring to their properties and methods of formation (the rock cycle).

Vocabulary Activity

The Rock Cycle

Rocks are constantly changing. Many change from one type of rock into another during a natural cycle called the rock cycle.

1. The word *minerals* has three syllables. How many syllables are in these words?

   magma _____

   lava _____

2. When two words appear together as a term, the first word acts as an adjective. It describes the second word in the term. Look at the term *rock cycle*. What is being described?

   _____

Lesson 3

What Is the Rock Cycle?

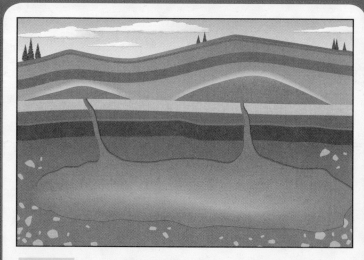

Magma is rock that flows deep inside Earth.

132

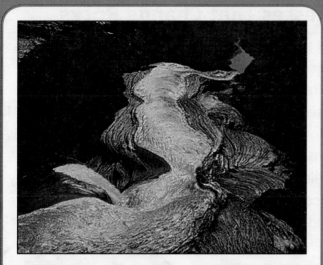

When a volcano erupts, **lava** flows onto Earth's surface.

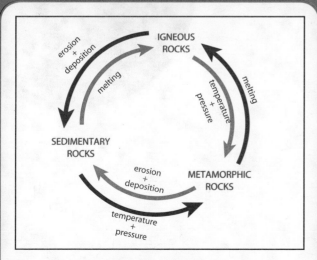

A rock changes into another rock as part of the **rock cycle**.

Hands-On Activity
Rock Cycle

Model the rock cycle using clay, glue, and two rocks.

1. Wear goggles, and ask a teacher for help. Break two rocks into pieces by dropping them on cement or stepping on them. What step in the rock cycle does this model?

_____

2. Now, roll the clay on top of the pieces of rock. Push it down. Cover the mixture with glue and let it dry. What kind of "rock" have you made?

_____

3. What would you need to do to turn the sedimentary rock into metamorphic rock?

_____

1. A **Cause** is something that makes another thing happen. An **Effect** is the thing that happens. Circle a cause of igneous rock formation. Underline an effect of large masses of rock pushing against each other.

2. Draw arrows from the lines to the magma and the lava. Write labels on the lines.

_____

_____

3. What does cooled and hardened lava produce?

_____

4. What happens when igneous rock is weathered?

_____

Processes That Change Rocks

Rock that is deep under Earth's surface becomes very hot. It melts and becomes soft or even liquid. The *molten*, or melted, rock inside Earth is called **magma**.

Molten rock that erupts from a volcano is called **lava**. Lava flows on the surface of Earth. When lava cools and hardens, it forms igneous rock.

The little bits of igneous rock that are worn away produce sediment. The process of wearing away rocks is called *weathering*. Weathering is one way in which rocks can be changed.

Rocks can also change through *erosion* (ee•ROH•zhuhn). In erosion, wind and running water move sediment from one place to another.

After sediment is eroded, it can be deposited, or set down. This is called *deposition* (dep•uh•ZISH•uhn). Sediment dropped by deposition can become sedimentary rock.

When large masses of rock push against each other, mountain ranges are formed. These changes cause the rock layers to look folded, broken, or tilted. Rock changes because of many things.

The Colorado River erodes sediment from upstream areas and moves it downstream. Some of the sediment is deposited at the river's mouth. The collected sediment forms a delta, a piece of new land.

✓ Concept Check

1. Fill in the chart. Tell what effects these three actions can have on rock.

Action	Effect on Rock
Weathering	
Erosion	
Deposition	

2. What can happen to sediment deposited by streams or the wind?

_____

3. What causes igneous rock to be changed into sedimentary rock?

_____

4. Draw to show how large masses of rock pushing against each other can change the land.

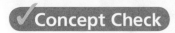

✓ Concept Check

1. A **Cause** is something that makes another thing happen. An **Effect** is the thing that happens. Look at the diagram of the rock cycle. Circle a cause of changes in rocks. Underline the effect of the cause you chose.

2. What is the rock cycle?

_____

_____

3. Fill in the chart. Use the diagram of the rock cycle to help you. The first one is done for you as an example.

Changes from	Changes into	Causes
Sedimentary	Metamorphic	temperature + pressure
Igneous	Igneous	
Sedimentary	Sedimentary	
Igneous	Metamorphic	
Metamorphic	Igneous	
Metamorphic	Sedimentary	

The Rock Cycle

Weathering, erosion, deposition, and high temperature and pressure can change rocks. Each of these processes is part of the rock cycle. The **rock cycle** is the endless process in which rocks change from one type to another.

Changes to rocks usually happen slowly. Rocks can take thousands of years to change. They can even take millions of years. Rocks follow different paths in the rock cycle. For example, any rock can be buried and melted. It can then cool to become new igneous rock.

Rock is constantly changing. These columns of rock used to be a volcano.

136

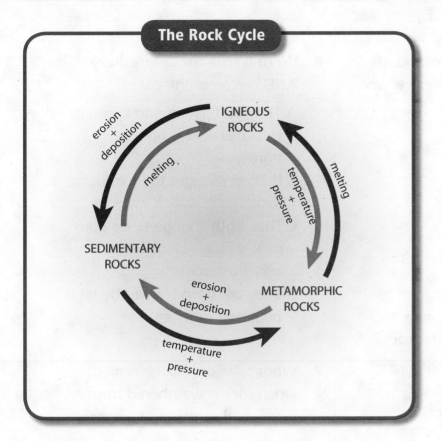

The Rock Cycle

IGNEOUS ROCKS

erosion + deposition

melting

temperature + pressure

melting

SEDIMENTARY ROCKS

erosion + deposition

temperature + pressure

METAMORPHIC ROCKS

Lesson Review

Complete these Cause and Effect statements.

1. Erupting causes magma to become _____.

2. _____ causes rocks to be worn away into sediment.

3. _____ carries sediment away from its source.

4. Weathering, erosion, deposition, heat, and pressure cause rocks to move through the _____.

Circle the letter in front of the best choice.

1. Which property is LEAST helpful for identifying minerals?

   A streak
   B color
   C hardness
   D luster

Use the Mohs Hardness Scale on page 122 to answer question 2.

2. Which mineral could scratch fluorite?

   A quartz
   B feldspar
   C calcite
   D topaz

3. What is luster?

   A the way a mineral breaks
   B the color of a mineral's powder
   C the measure of how hard it is to scratch another mineral
   D the way a mineral reflects light

4. A rock breaks along a smooth, flat surface. What property does it have?

   A cleavage
   B fracture
   C luster
   D hardness

Use the diagram on page 133 to answer questions 5 and 6.

5. What causes igneous rock to change to metamorphic rock?

   A melting and then hardening
   B heat and pressure
   C weathering and erosion
   D weathering only

6. What is true for sedimentary AND metamorphic rocks?

   A They both change to igneous rock by melting and then hardening.
   B Neither changes to igneous rock.
   C They both change to igneous rock through weathering and erosion.
   D They are both formed by high heat and pressure.

7. What type of rock is formed when rock is weathered to small pieces and cemented together?

   A metamorphic
   B igneous
   C sedimentary
   D small-grain

8. What determines whether an igneous rock will have large or small crystals?

A size of original rock
B temperature only
C time and size
D temperature and time

9. If you can see the minerals in a rock, it is said to have

A small-grain texture.
B coarse-grain texture.
C crystals.
D stripes.

10. What kind of rock can have stripes of melted minerals?

A sedimentary
B sediment
C igneous
D metamorphic

11. Granite is made underground and has large crystals. What kind of rock is it?

A sedimentary
B sediment
C igneous
D metamorphic

12. Look at the picture of the rock cycle. Fill in the blanks to tell what kinds of rocks are made.

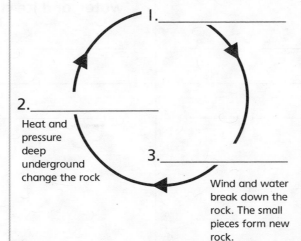

Melted rock reaches Earth's surface through a volcano and cools.

1. _____

2. _____

Heat and pressure deep underground change the rock

3. _____

Wind and water break down the rock. The small pieces form new rock.

13. Name one visible property of each of the three kinds of rocks.

_____

_____

_____

14. Look back to the question you wrote on page 112. Do you have an answer for your question? Tell what you learned that helps you understand rocks and minerals.

_____

_____

_____

_____

_____

_____

_____

_____

Waves, Wind, Water, and Ice

In this unit, you will learn about things that change Earth's surface. You will learn more about the process of weathering, and how moving water shapes the land. What do you know about these topics? What questions do you have?

Thinking Ahead

Write the names of three things that change Earth's surface.

_____

_____

Name three things that cause weathering.

_____

_____

How do you think rivers and erosion are related?

_____

_____

Write a question you have about how waves, wind, water, and ice change Earth's surface.

_____

_____

Recording What You Learn

◄ On this page, record what you learn as you read the unit.

Lesson 1

Write the names of two things that change Earth's surface quickly.

_____

Write the names of two things that change Earth's surface slowly.

_____

Lesson 2

Number the steps in the drawing below. Tell how water is weathering rock in Step 1.

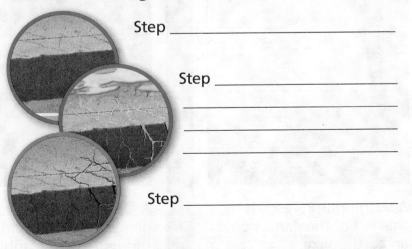

Step _____

Step _____

_____

_____

_____

Step _____

Lesson 3

Name two sources of sand on beaches.

1. _____

_____

_____

_____

2. _____

_____

_____

_____

5.a *Students know* that some changes in the Earth are due to slow processes such as erosion, and some changes due to rapid processes such as landslides, volcanic eruptions, and earthquakes.

Vocabulary Activity

Earth's Changing Surface

In this lesson, you'll learn that some changes to Earth's surface happen quickly. Others happen slowly.

I. Show that the words *earthquake* and *landslide* are compound words.

_____

2. You may have heard the words *creep*, *volcano*, *lava*, and *dune* used before. Write a sentence for each word.

Word	Sentence
Creep	
Volcano	
Lava	
Dune	

Lesson **1**

What Causes Changes to Earth's Surface?

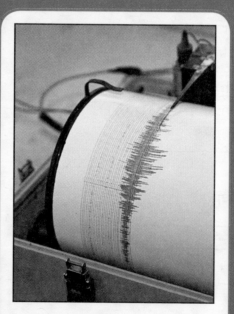

A seismograph records the shaking of the earth from an **earthquake**.

A **landslide** can be very dangerous. Rock and soil suddenly slip downhill.

Creep can slowly block mountain roads.

This mountain is a **volcano** that was formed by molten rock.

Lava can flow quickly down a volcano's side.

A **dune** can change shape when the wind blows.

Hands-On Activity
Modeling Dunes

Do this activity outdoors.

1. Put on goggles. Fill a box lid with sand. Make a sand dune. Draw a picture of what your dune looks like.

2. Now, pour a little water down the side of your dune. What happens to the sand?

3. Draw a picture of what your dune looks like now.

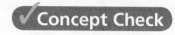

✓ Concept Check

1. You **Compare** how things are alike. You **Contrast** how things are different. Compare and contrast landslides and creep.

	Same	**Different**
Landslides		
Creep		

2. What causes earthquakes?

_____

3. Fill in the chart. Tell whether each change is caused by an earthquake or a landslide.

Change	Cause
Cracks open in Earth's surface.	
Rocks and dirt rush down a hillside.	
Parts of the ground tilt up.	
Mountains can rise higher.	
Piles of dirt are left at the bottom of a hill.	
Buildings can break and fall down.	

Earthquakes and Landslides

Giant slabs of rock move in Earth's crust. An **earthquake** is the shaking of Earth's crust. Shaking is caused by sudden movements of the slabs.

Earthquakes cause fast changes in Earth's surface. Huge cracks open. Parts of the ground tilt up. Mountains can rise higher. Buildings can break and fall down.

A landslide also happens quickly. A **landslide** is when rocks and dirt rush down a hillside. Piles of dirt and rocks are left at the bottom. Holes are left where dirt, trees, rocks, and houses used to be.

The ground moved along the crack. The movement was part of an earthquake.

Some changes to Earth's surface happen slowly. **Creep** is when dirt and rocks move very slowly down a hillside. The dirt and rocks can move things in their path. Over time, fence posts on a hill become tilted. Over a long time, creep can even flatten a hill.

Creep caused the curves of these tree trunks.

1. Underline the sentence that defines the word *creep*.

2. You see a tilted fence post on a hill. What most likely caused this?

_____

3. Contrast the ways earthquakes and creep change Earth's surface.

_____

_____

4. Circle the sentence that tells what might happen if creep goes unnoticed over a long time.

_____

1. You **Compare** how things are alike. You **Contrast** how things are different. Compare the ways volcanoes and glaciers affect Earth's surface.

_____

_____

_____

2. Fill in the chart to show harmful and helpful changes a volcano can cause.

Harmful	Helpful

3. Name three things that can change Earth's surface.

_____

_____

_____

Volcanoes

A **volcano** is a mountain formed by the flow of lava. Lava flows from a crack in Earth's surface. **Lava** is molten, or melted, rock at Earth's surface.

Volcanoes cause harmful or helpful changes. The ash from a volcanic eruption can break down into rich soil. Lava from volcanoes in the sea can form new land. Lava can also destroy homes and cities.

Mount Shasta is a large volcano in California.

Ice and Wind

Glaciers are huge sheets of ice. The slow movement of glaciers changes Earth's surface. Glaciers make valleys wider and gradually scoop holes in Earth.

Wind changes Earth's surface, too. A **dune** forms when wind blows sand into a mound. Dunes are common in the desert.

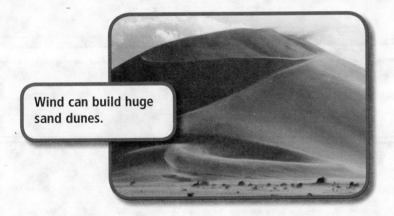

Wind can build huge sand dunes.

Complete these Compare and Contrast statements.

1. _____ and landslides both cause fast changes in Earth's surface.

2. _____ causes change to Earth's surface more slowly than a landslide does.

3. Volcanoes can cause both harmful and _____ changes.

4. Glaciers scoop _____ in Earth. Wind blows sand into a _____.

5.b *Students know* material processes including freezing, thawing, and the growth of roots cause rocks to break down into smaller pieces.

Vocabulary Activity

Weathering

Weathering is one way Earth's surface is changed. Different things can cause weathering.

1. When two words are together as one term, the first word acts as an adjective. Fill in the chart below to show the two kinds of weathering.

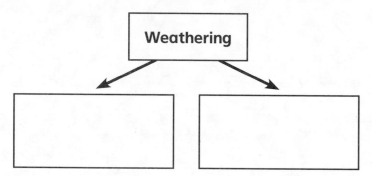

Weathering

2. As a verb, the word *soil* means "to get dirty." What does the word *soil* mean as a noun?

_____

_____

_____

Lesson **2**

What Causes Weathering?

VOCABULARY

weathering
soil
mechanical weathering
chemical weathering

Weathering breaks down rock. It can create holes in rocks.

Weathering helps create **soil**. Soil is a mixture of weathered rock, bits of dead things, water, and air.

1. Look for signs of weathering in your community. Examples include broken sidewalks or rusty objects. Draw pictures of the weathered objects. List what you found.

_____

_____

_____

_____

2. On a sheet of posterboard, make two columns. Label one "Mechanical Weathering." Label the other "Chemical Weathering."

3. Tape your pictures to the poster board. Separate the examples into the correct columns. What is the difference between mechanical weathering and chemical weathering?

_____

_____

_____

_____

Wind and weather break down rock by **mechanical weathering**.

Water breaks down rock by **chemical weathering**.

1. A **Cause** makes something happen. An **Effect** is the thing that happens. Circle one cause of mechanical weathering. Underline an effect of weathering.

2. Use the space below to draw before and after pictures. Show a rock before it is weathered. Then show it after.

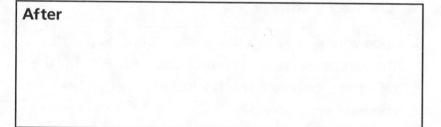

Before

After

Mechanical Weathering

Weathering is part of the rock cycle. Rocks break down into smaller pieces, called sediment. **Soil** is a mixture of weathered rock, the remains of dead organisms, water, and air.

Mechanical weathering breaks rock into smaller pieces. Ice, water, wind, and temperature changes all cause rock to weather.

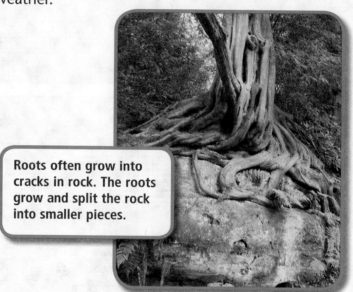

Roots often grow into cracks in rock. The roots grow and split the rock into smaller pieces.

Water runs into cracks in rocks and freezes. Water expands as it freezes. The cracks get wider. The water thaws. This happens again and again. Over time, the rocks can break apart.

Rocks get a little bigger when heated. They get a little smaller when cooled. Repeated heating and cooling weakens some rocks. When the rocks are weakened, they crack or break.

Water in the form of ice can break down rock and concrete.

◀ Water runs into a crack.

◀ The water freezes and becomes ice. Frozen water takes up more space than liquid water. It pushes against the sides of the crack.

◀ The crack becomes wider and breaks the concrete or rock.

1. What can cause mechanical weathering?

_____

_____

2. Fill in the chart. Tell the effect of the weathering method.

Weathered by	Effect
Water freezing in cracks	
Repeated heating and cooling	

3. Why does repeated heating and cooling cause rocks to break?

_____

4. Number the statements to put them in order.

____ The water freezes and becomes ice. Frozen water takes up more space than liquid water. It pushes against the sides of the crack.

____ Water runs into a crack.

____ The crack becomes wider and breaks the concrete or rock.

1. A **Cause** makes something happen. An **Effect** is the thing that happens. Circle the sentence that explains what causes rock to change its chemical makeup. Underline an effect of chemical weathering.

2. Complete the equation for chemical weathering.

   Water + oxygen + _____ + minerals in the rock =

   _____

3. You know that metal can rust. Rocks can rust, too. Why do some rocks get rusty?

   _____

   _____

   _____

Chemical Weathering

Water breaks down rock by **chemical weathering**. Water and gases in the air cause most chemical weathering. Water, oxygen, and pollution can mix with minerals in the rock. This changes the chemical makeup of the rock. The rock breaks down.

Some minerals contain iron. Oxygen in the air can combine with this iron. This creates rust on the outer layer of the rock.

Sinkholes can be formed by chemical weathering. This is a 15-story-deep sinkhole in Florida.

Lesson Review

Complete these Cause and Effect statements.

1. Changes in temperature can cause _____.

2. Freezing causes water to _____.

3. Cold causes rocks to get a little _____.

4. Water and gases in the air cause most _____ _____.

Vocabulary Activity

Moving Water

The vocabulary words describe different ways water can change land.

1. The chart below shows two vocabulary words and defines the parts that make up each word. Put them together to tell what the vocabulary word means.

Vocabulary Word	Root: Meaning	Meaning of Vocabulary Word
Erosion	Erode: wear away *-sion*: process of	
Deposition	Deposit: to put or set down *-tion*: process of	
Transport	*Trans-*: across or through Port: to carry	

Lesson **3**

How Does Moving Water Shape the Land?

VOCABULARY

erosion
transport
runoff
deposition

Erosion formed this gully. The dirt and sediment were washed away.

These sandbars were made by **transport**. Sediment is *transported* from place to place by water.

© Harcourt

Runoff is water that flows over the land without sinking in.

This delta was formed by **deposition**. The river drops off sediment as it slows down.

1. Put soil into a plastic tub. Build up all the soil into a "mountain" in one end of the tub.

2. Pour water very slowly onto the top of your mountain. Observe how the water flows down the sides.

3. Then pour water very quickly onto the top of your mountain. Observe what happens to the soil. Draw what your mountain looks like now.

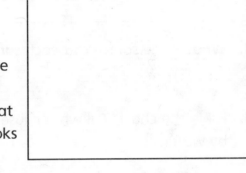

4. Answer the questions.

• After doing Step 3, is your mountain bigger or smaller than it was in Step 1? _____

• What happened to the soil during Step 2 and Step 3?

_____

• In Step 1, there was soil only at one end of the tub. After Step 3, how much of the tub has soil in it?

_____

1. The **Main Idea** of these two pages is <u>Moving water changes the land.</u> **Details** tell more about the main idea. Underline two details about how water changes the land.

2. How are deltas formed?

_____

3. What is the source of beach sand?

_____

4. Fill in the chart. Tell what causes each change made by water.

Change	Cause
Sediment is moved to rivers.	
Deltas form.	
Beaches form.	
Cliffs break into pieces.	

Rivers Shape the Land

Erosion moves sediment from one place to another. This changes Earth's surface.

Rivers erode landforms and change them. Rivers contain runoff. **Runoff** is water that flows over land without sinking in. Runoff transports, or moves, sediment to rivers.

As rivers slow down they drop sediment. This is called **deposition**. Deposition forms landforms such as deltas at the mouths of rivers. Deposition also leaves sediment inside curves along the river banks.

 How are deltas formed?

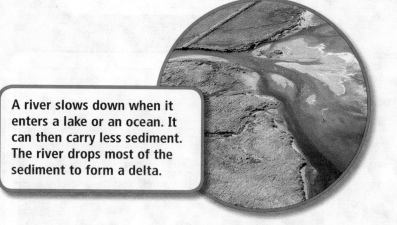

A river slows down when it enters a lake or an ocean. It can then carry less sediment. The river drops most of the sediment to form a delta.

Ocean Waves Shape the Land

Waves are another cause of weathering and erosion. Large ocean waves pound the coastlines. Over time, the pounding breaks the rock into pieces.

Deposition on coasts forms beaches. Waves and ocean currents pick up sediment from weathered cliffs. Rivers also drop sediment into the sea. The ocean deposits sediment from all these sources on the shore. The deposition becomes beach sand.

 What is the source of beach sand?

Waves hitting cliffs are a cause of weathering.

Complete this Main Idea statement.

1. Moving _____ shapes the land.

Complete these Detail statements.

2. _____ is water that moves sediments to rivers.

3. Deposition forms landforms such as _____.

4. Rivers drop _____ as they enter the sea.

© Harcourt

Circle the letter in front of the best choice.

1. A statue is covered with rust. This is an example of

   A chemical weathering.
   B mechanical weathering.
   C climatic weathering.
   D erosion of sediment.

2. Which is an example of mechanical weathering?

   A sinkhole
   B rusted rocks
   C tree roots cracking rock
   D pollution causing the makeup of rock to change

3. What forms dunes?

   A water
   B ice
   C wind
   D landslides

4. Which changes Earth's surface quickly?

   A erosion
   B creep
   C glacier
   D landslide

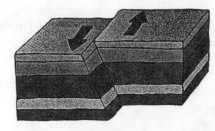

5. What MOST LIKELY caused these giant slabs of Earth's crust to move?

   A mechanical weathering
   B earthquake
   C creep
   D volcano

6. What MOST LIKELY caused this tree to tilt downhill?

   A mechanical weathering
   B earthquake
   C creep
   D volcano

7. Which of these does NOT weather rock?

   A water
   B ice
   C land
   D plant roots

8. What does erosion do?

   A break rocks

   B change temperatures

   C rust metal

   D move sediment

9. Why do rivers drop sediment?

   A because they slow down

   B because it gets too heavy

   C because the sediment stops
   moving

   D because they speed up

10. Which is NOT a source of beach
sand?

   A sediment from cliffs

   B sediment from rivers

   C sediment from the ocean

   D sediment from lakes

11. What is deposition?

   A carrying of sediment

   B dropping of sediment

   C rocks that have been worn down

   D water that runs over land

12. Explain how a landslide changes
Earth's surface.

_____

_____

_____

13. How can water break a concrete
road?

_____

_____

_____

14. Look back at the question you
asked on page 141. Do you have
an answer for your question?
Tell what you learned that helps
you understand how waves,
wind, water, and ice change
Earth's surface.

_____

_____

_____

_____

_____